QUEER HAUNTS

This anthology is dedicated to
Gay Authors' Workshop,
this year celebrating
Its thirty-fifth anniversary.

QUEER HAUNTS

edited by

G. Abel-Watters

Paradise Press

First published in Great Britain in 2003 by
Paradise Press, BM Box 5700, London WC1N 3XX.
www.paradisepress.org.uk

Copyright © GAW 2003

This second edition published in 2013
with additional stories:
Beyond the Grave, by Donald West
The Inn, by Brian Burton
Colour Him Gay by Gail Morris
Whitebeech, by Miles Martlett
And Twelfth Night, by Alice Windsor
Which are all copyright © 2013

A CIP catalogue record for this book
is available from the British Library.

ISBN 978-1-904585-58-9

Printed and bound in Great Britain by
Lightning Source UK Ltd, Milton Keynes.

Cover design by Mike Lorenzini.

CONTENTS

Introduction

G Abel-Watters

Stories of ghosts, the supernatural or unexplained happenings have been told throughout the world, probably since humankind first developed language. Whether passed down orally or read around the fire to while away a dark night or stormy afternoon, tales of the unknown and unknowable have always found a ready audience. We all relish the chill down the spine, the sharp intake of breath, or the nervous laugh such tales induce.

Ghosts, and supernatural manifestations, may seem less credible as we survey life from the vantage-point of the twenty-first century, and it is noticeable in this collection that such ghosts as appear are in general quite untraditional.

But in spite of huge advances in knowledge, and manipulation of the world in which we find ourselves, there is still plenty that defies explanation, while the continuing popularity of horror films and television series such as The X-Files demonstrates that people are as fascinated as ever by the unusual or outlandish.

While there have been any number of ghost stories, there are relatively few specifically lesbian or gay ones. This, indeed, mirrors much of life, where queer experience has long been hidden away in a largely heterosexual world – as in one of these stories, in which the heterosexual ghost has become a part of folklore, while the gay ghost, like the doings of Uncle Hector in another of the stories, is simply not talked about.

This collection is partly a step to redressing some of the imbalance mentioned above, but most of all, it is a set of stories for us all to enjoy that are both close to home and inexplicable. Whether you read this volume with scepticism, boldness or trepidation, you are sure to find the stories intriguing and, dare I say, haunting.

THE CALL

Michael Harth

Though he was a compulsive browser in antiquarian bookshops, and had over the years picked up a number of interesting items, a few especially so, James had never for a moment dreamed that he would come across what he now held in his hands. The marked price was unbelievably low for such a treasure, and the excitement of finding something so rare and comparatively inexpensive overcame his natural caution, so that, once a second glance had confirmed that the book was indeed what it seemed, he didn't try to haggle, as was his usual practice, for fear that the bookseller would say 'I'm afraid this is wrongly marked, sir' and name a price far above what he would have been prepared to pay.

But nothing of the sort happened; he left the shop with his heart beating wildly, and hurried home to subject his purchase to a closer examination than he had deemed sensible on the premises. This confirmed that he had not been mistaken: it was indeed a copy of the *Liber Logaeth*, written in the Enochian language, which neither he nor anyone else he knew of was able to interpret convincingly, though there had of course been a number of attempts, none of which he considered had proved their case.

He did rather wonder why something so obviously old and, at the least, unusual, was being sold at such a relatively low price, but assumed that the bookseller hadn't known just how valuable the book was. Maybe he had got hold of it cheaply, and was content with a reasonable profit. Certainly there were very few people who would be able to recognise it as being written in the Enochian script, which was different from that of any other language: probably the bookseller had assumed that it was merely some language he had not come across, and so of little interest, pricing it accordingly.

James, however, knew that the contents of this book were supposed to have been dictated to Dr John Dee, the famous scholar and magician who lived during the reign of Queen Elizabeth, was her court mathematician, and was also reputed to have spied for her. Dee, not himself being psychic, had employed others as mediums, the most notable of them being Edward Kelley. The pair had held regular séances, during which they believed they were being communicated with by angels. However James, whose parents had been staunch Christians, and who still adhered to the main tenets of that religion even though he was not a churchgoer, was positive they were nothing of the sort. Just what they were he was less certain about.

The language was called Enochian because of the angelic connection, since the apocryphal Book of Enoch tells of angels walking the earth and forming forbidden liaisons with humans. James had been working from a transcript of part of what the two men had recorded, though his attempts at decoding it had been hampered by not knowing how reliable his copy was.

Considering his views, there was some degree of inconsistency in the fact of James' working on the manuscript, since the part he had gave eight of the eighteen calls or keys by which the angels could be summoned. He knew they had been used for this purpose by a number of Golden Dawn adepts, among them Aleister Crowley, who he was also aware was by no means the charlatan some supposed. What success they had had James didn't know: even if they had thought they had achieved their objective, they could have been hallucinating or deceiving themselves in one way or another.

Since he was convinced that the version they used was inaccurate, he rather doubted whether they would have got anywhere. James wasn't even sure what he would do with his revised version when he had finished it; whether he would try it out, or remain satisfied with the knowledge that he, unlike all the others he knew who shared his interest, possessed an accurate version.

He didn't have time that evening to start the thorough methodical examination he was planning, but he couldn't resist turning to the page which showed the table he had been working on:

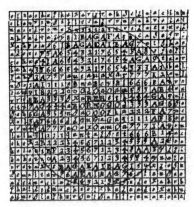

In the centre was a circle, which nestled itself exactly within the central 9 (3×3) smaller 7×7 tables. Around the inside of this ring was a circle of numbers, this time from 1 to 9, and he looked immediately at the bottom left part of the circle. To his delight, he saw that the o and e in his copy were here the 8 and 9 he had reasoned were necessary to keep the pattern.

He was certain now that he had an accurate copy, instead of the one riddled with errors he had been working from. It was going to be a hard slog which would require every ounce of his concentration, he thought with satisfaction, so he decided to delay it until he had dealt with anything that needed fairly immediate attention, after which he should be able to shut himself up with his new possession for, he hoped, several days.

But that night he experienced an extremely vivid dream, and he was still feeling uneasy when he sat down to a lighter breakfast than usual. Taking a firm grip on what was no doubt an over-active imagination, he decided that it was because finding the book was far and away the most exciting thing that had happened to him for years, even thought the book itself hadn't featured in it.

It was really more like a nightmare than a dream, though nothing unpleasant had actually happened. He had merely found himself walking along a corridor, unlocking a great heavy oaken door, and going inside the room, which proved to be a library. All the books looked old-fashioned: there was no suggestion of modern covers, so he assumed that either he was dreaming about the past, or the library collection contained only old books.

It was all harmless enough in itself: there had been nothing to account for the feeling of dread that had accompanied the dream, and still lingered when he woke up, and was no doubt the reason why he found himself strangely unwilling to start work on the book, and on one or another pretext he postponed looking at it. Then the next night he had the same dream, but this time it continued to the point where he found himself walking over to one particular shelf and taking down a book, which, he knew as he did it, would prove to be the book he had just acquired.

He was powerless to stop himself opening it, but as he turned over the pages he could see they were all blank. This was a definite relief, for though there was a possibility that they might provide some sort of clue which would help him in interpreting the actual book which he had in his study, he found that he didn't actually want to know what a translation would reveal.

But on the next night following, as he dreamed that he once again stood there, with the book open in front of him, the pages began to fill with characters in what he knew only too well was Enochian script: he didn't examined them closely enough to be sure whether they were the same, but nonetheless he found something extremely discomfiting about them. The sense of being taken on a journey he had no wish to make had become too much to endure passively, so he went to see his doctor. Dr. Fellowes was not one of the 'Pull yourself together' school: wiser and with wider sympathies than many of his profession, he could see at once that James was under enormous strain.

Fortunately James could well afford a private consultation – if he had had to wait for an appointment through the NHS, it would no doubt have been too late to be of any use. As it was, it proved difficult to arrange anything, but finally a Dr Jenkins, who was due to go on holiday that evening, and so had arranged a lighter workload than usual, agreed to see him after his last patient, However, even though these days a visit to see a psychiatrist didn't carry the sort of stigma it would have had years ago, he was still embarrassed about it and feeling slightly guilty about having upset holiday arrangements, so he played down the urgency he felt, with the result that he ended up being reassured that the dreams were merely due to his having got so excited over his find, and thus nothing to worry about.

Even when driving back from the consultation, he was cursing himself for not having stressed the fact that he felt threatened in the dreams. He even thought about turning back to see him again, but he told himself the man would probably have left by the time he got there. He did his best to stay awake that night, sitting up in his armchair and reading instead of going to bed, but after a while he couldn't keep awake any longer, and drifted off.

This time the book opened up in front of him, and he began to read aloud from the pages. His voice sounded entirely different from how he normally heard it, deeper and more resonant, and the syllables reverberated with power through the vast space in which he was standing. He had no idea what the words were: none of them bore any resemblance to anything he was familiar with. Nonetheless he read them out confidently, each word dropping into the silence with ominous portent.

There were only a few dozen words on the page, and he soon came to the end of them. He didn't want to turn the page, but he could feel himself being urged to do so. The struggle was sufficient to wake him: he was sweating, and still had a lingering sensation of dread. He took a shower and made himself a drink, after which he felt better, so then he went to bed, since otherwise he would be exhausted on the morrow, and so far as he knew he didn't dream any more that night.

The next night was very much the same. Once again he read the incantation, for that was what he assumed it must be, from the book, but this time, once he had finished reading from the page shown, the page was turned by some unseen hand.

Mercifully, the new page was blank, but it began to fill with characters as he looked at it. The feeling of apprehension this created was strong enough to help him to force himself awake before the process had finished.

He had a horrible feeling that all this was leading up to something, and he was positive it would be something unpleasant or worse. So the next morning, as soon as he had finished his breakfast, he went into his study and took down the book. He went through the pages slowly, looking to see if they reminded him of what he had seen in his dreams, but though they did have a certain familiarity, he couldn't be sure. But then, as he went through them for the second time, he found himself stopping at one of the pages, and as he gazed, his vision blurred. When he could see clearly again, he found he could read the letters.

The words so shown were in no language he knew, but nonetheless he was able to pronounce them and, as he began to read them out, he found he was repeating the incantation of his dream. The realisation made him stop short, in the middle of a word, and he hastily shut the book and put it away. He had plenty of other things to get on with, but all day, whatever he was doing, he found his mind returning to the book, and he experienced the desire to complete the incantation.

At first he dismissed it easily enough, but as the day wore on the feeling became more pressing, and when he found himself going back to the study without having actually intended to go there, he began to panic, put his coat on, and went out for a walk.

Once in the fresh air, and with the sun every so often showing its face through the clouds, he was able to relax, and gave himself a good talking-to, telling himself that he was letting the book prey on his mind too much. He had several other projects that had to be completed sometime that year: it would obviously be wise to get on with them, and only return to deciphering the book's language when he was fresher.

By the time he returned he felt more like his old self, and for the rest of the day he resolutely kept his mind on other matters, so that he went to bed in a better frame of mind, telling his subconscious he didn't want any more dreams, and especially not about his recent acquisition.

It seemed to work, for he dropped off easily enough, and his sleep was untroubled. But a while later he woke to find himself in his study, with the book in his hand. As if in a dream, he saw himself turning the pages till he arrived at the twelfth call, while when he looked the characters were no longer a script that he could only decipher with the aid of his painstakingly compiled dictionary: he could read them and did, saying the words aloud.

Their correct pronunciation was a matter of dispute among scholars, but he seemed to know instinctively how to say them, each syllable resounding as if in a great cave rather than his little study. The air began to vibrate, and there was a sound as of beating wings, which at last roused him to a sense of imminent danger. Even so, it was only by exerting every ounce of will-power he could muster that he managed to stop himself reading, and shut the book.

Once that was done, he collapsed into his chair, exhausted. He didn't dare go back to sleep, but sat in the chair, keeping himself awake with cups of coffee, until dawn broke. He had already decided the book had to go, and as soon as it was light he dressed, put on an overcoat, for the morning was chilly, and drove to the riverside, a few miles away. He had hoped that the spot he had chosen would be deserted at this early hour, but there was a young man walking along the riverside path. James had been celibate for the past twelve months or so, and normally he was a compulsive window-shopper, but now he was so intent on his errand that he didn't even bother to appraise the fellow's attractions, which was his usual substitute for sex.

Not until the fellow had disappeared from view did James take out the book: then he gazed at it for a few moments. It seemed crazy to be throwing away such a valuable and possibly unique object, and he hesitated, but the remembrance of his dreams hardened his resolution, and with the most powerful swing he could manage he threw the book out into the middle of the water, waiting until he saw it sink. Then he went home with a much lighter heart.

But that night he again woke to find himself in his study with the book in his hand, apparently unaffected by its immersion, and it took even more effort than the time before to shut it. The sense of impending doom was stronger now: he knew he had to get rid of the book, but obviously ordinary means were not enough: it had to be completely destroyed.

So he lit the fire in his study and, once it was burning well, piled on the coals till he had a mass of incandescent embers. Then he held the book with a pair of tongs and thrust it into the flames, keeping it there until he had seen the pages shrivel and blacken. His hands were scorched in the process, but that was a small matter besides the relief he felt afterwards.

It was short-lasting. When he awoke later that night to find the book once again in his hands, clearly none the worse for his attempt to destroy it, he accepted his fate. It was already open, and he read aloud the call. Soon the syllables, resonant as before, were accompanied by the same sound as of beating wings, but he read on, terrified yet resigned.

He had no idea what sort of creature it was that waited at the twelfth gate, so clearly impatient to enter the world of men, but he doubted whether its intentions were benevolent. The sounds grew louder and he felt a sensation of immense heat, as if he were in a desert with the midday sun blazing down. A little later, and he saw it. He had time to wonder how Dee and Kelley could ever have imagined that it was an angel.

A BIT OF FUN

Kathryn Bell

'We changed our minds,' Karen said. 'We're not doing the music thing tonight.'

'Great,' Elspeth thought. So the half-hour she had spent selecting a disc to bring had been a complete waste of time. She had quickly narrowed the choice to the Rolling Stones or Vivaldi, but taken twenty minutes to make her final decision in favour of the latter. Still, it wasn't as bad as the time the gang had announced a fancy-dress evening with a Nursery theme; Elspeth had gone as Contrary Mary, in ankle-length print frock and beribboned straw hat, carrying a basket of 'silver bells' she had painstakingly made from milk-bottle tops and pipe-cleaner stems, to be met by the crowd in jeans and T-shirts exclaiming 'We cancelled the fancy dress …'

'Didn't anyone tell you? Eileen was supposed …'

'No, I thought *Karen* was telling you …'

Elspeth sat on the arm of the two-seater sofa which contained Mags and Eileen. Joanne was explaining: 'Jessica had this great idea for a fun thing to do tonight. She got it out of a book her aunt gave her.'

Jessica's Aunt Lil had recently moved to sheltered accommodation and, finding herself short of space, had parcelled out her surplus possessions among her family. Jessica had come in for most of the books, including a large volume entitled *How To Do Just About Anything*. As well as the usual advice on mending fuses and replacing tap washers, it gave instructions on how to make and operate a ouija board.

'I thought we could try it out,' Jessica enthused. 'Maybe we can contact somebody.'

Elspeth noticed that the small lettered squares of paper had already been laid out on the dining-room table, and an upturned tumbler placed in the middle.

'And does it tell you how to get rid of unwelcome visitors?' she enquired.

'Uh – how do you mean?' Jessica was puzzled. 'There's nothing like that in the instructions.'

'Try looking under "entity",' Elspeth suggested. 'Or maybe "exorcism".'

'I hope you're not going to be a spoilsport,' said Karen.

'Do you think you could contact Delia for me?' asked Eileen. 'I want to ask her if she knows what went wrong with my *crème brûlée* on Sunday.'

'Don't be silly, of course I can't contact Delia,' said Jessica.

'Oh. The other one, then. The dishy one. Nigella.'

'I can't contact the dishy one either. They're alive, see. The ouija can only contact dead people.'

'Only *dead* people? What's the use of that?'

'Oh, I don't know,' Elspeth put in. 'Mrs Beeton might be able to help you.'

'There, you're not going to be a spoilsport after all. You're getting into the spirit of it,' said Karen.

'Spirit, that's good,' said Joanne, laughing. 'Have a mint.' She handed round a bag of mint imperials.

'No, ta,' Mags passed the bag on. 'Don't like mints.'

'They're not very strong mints,' Joanne said.

'Doesn't matter. I don't like mints *at all*. Sorry,' said Mags with an apologetic smile.

'I don't *want* to be a spoilsport,' said Elspeth. 'I just wonder if you've thought about what we might be letting ourselves in for.'

Five questioning faces turned towards her. No one spoke.

'What I imagine it could be like,' Elspeth struggled to articulate her misgivings, 'is, suppose there's a place outside the world we know of, and it's all dark and cold;

19

there's nothing interesting there, nothing to look at or to do, and the – er- beings there, they're wandering about, looking for a way to get into our world, where there's light and noise and people. And when somebody is using something like a ouija board, that opens a sort of gate, and the things from outside could find it and come through.'

'You mean like ghosts?' Karen asked.

'I don't know. They might be ghosts, or they might be something completely different; elementals or devils or something.'

'Lighten up, Elspeth,' said Jessica. 'It's only meant to be a bit of fun.'

'How do you spell "exorcism"?' asked Joanne, leafing through *How To Do Just About Anything.*

'All right, I give up,' said Elspeth. 'Let's have fun.' She sat down at the dining-room table, followed by the others.

'Now what? Do we join hands?' Karen asked.

'No,' said Jessica, 'we each put one finger on the glass.'

'Shouldn't we put the light out?' asked Mags.

'Of course not,' said Jessica. 'We wouldn't be able to read the messages if we did.'

Each woman placed one finger on the tumbler. 'Is there anyone there?' Jessica asked.

Nothing happened.

'Okay, you want fun, I'll give you fun', Elspeth thought. It took surprisingly little pressure to make the glass move towards the square of paper on which the word 'yes' was written.

Karen squealed in excitement. Jessica asked 'Who are you?'

Elspeth gently steered the glass to A, then to N.

'Ann? Could it be Ann Somebody? What was Mrs Beeton's first name?' asked Eileen.

'Isabella, I think,' said Elspeth, moving the glass to O. It had occurred to her to pretend to be Mrs Beeton, but as she didn't even know what *crème brûlée* was, she felt it would be unfair to stain Mrs Beeton's reputation with Elspeth's ignorance. She moved the glass back to N, then to the centre of the table.

'Anon? What does that mean?' said Eileen.

'Means whoever it is doesn't want to give their name,' said Jessica. 'Strange, that, it's not supposed to happen.'

'So what do we do now?'

'Have you got a message for anyone here?' Jessica asked.

Elspeth moved the glass to 'yes'.

'Who is the message for?'

The shortest name would be easiest. Elspeth moved the glass to M, but when she tried to move it to A, to spell MAGS, she felt an odd sensation. The glass was resisting her. She did not dare exert much pressure in case she might be detected by the others, so she relaxed her finger and let the glass move where it wanted. It slid to E, then swiftly on to G, then returned to the middle of the table.

Mags snatched her finger away from the glass and stood up, looking agitated. 'I don't want to play this stupid game any more,' she said.

'But the message might be for you,' said Jessica. 'Meg might be a mistake for Mags.'

'I said I don't want to play any more,' Mags said.

'*Now* who's being a spoilsport?' said Karen.

'It's okay, Mags,' said Joanne. 'Tell you what, why don't you go and put on a pot of coffee? You know where everything is. Two packets of biscuits in the vegetable rack.'

Mags went into the kitchen.

'Meg isn't here,' said Jessica. 'Have you a message for anyone else?'

The glass did not move. Control seemed to have been returned to Elspeth. Deciding on the next shortest name, she moved the glass to K, then A, R, E and N.

'What is your message for Karen?' Jessica asked.

Elspeth was beginning to wish she had never started this. She slid the glass to A, then S, then K.

'Ask?' said Karen. 'What the hell does that mean?'

'I think it means you have to ask it a question,' said Jessica.

'Right,' said Karen. 'When will I meet the woman of my dreams?'

Elspeth made the glass say SOON.

Karen giggled. 'What's her name?'

EDNA, the glass spelled.

'Edna? What sort of name is that? It's an old lady's name, the name of somebody's granny,' Karen complained.

'How old is Edna?' Jessica asked.

Elspeth, careless from over-confidence, pushed a bit too hard moving the glass towards the square marked with the number 9.

'Somebody's doing this on purpose,' Joanne exclaimed, taking her finger off the glass.

Karen and Jessica took their fingers off too, just as Elspeth slid the glass over to number 3.

'It's Elspeth!' said Eileen, 'I felt her pushing it.'

'Right, that's it; you're barred,' said Jessica.

Mags came in with the coffee.

'Silly sort of game anyway,' said Eileen.

'Only if people won't take it seriously,' said Jessica, looking pointedly at Elspeth.

'I don't know,' said Elspeth, 'first you say it's a bit of fun, then you blame me for not taking it seriously. Make up your mind.'

Later, washing up the coffee mugs and plates as atonement for her crime, Elspeth was joined by Mags.

'I'm glad it was you messing about back then,' Mags said. 'There was only one person who ever called me 'Meg', and he was absolutely the last person I would want to get a message from.'

'Who?'

'My uncle. He died about ten years ago. He ... wasn't a very nice man.'

Elspeth decided not to tell Mags about the sensation of outside control that had made her spell 'Meg' instead of 'Mags'.

Eileen lived in the next street to Elspeth's, so as usual Elspeth drove her home.

'I think Jessica was a bit fed up with you for spoiling her game,' said Eileen.

'Yes, and I was only trying to make it interesting,' said Elspeth. 'Not much fun if we'd just all sat round the stupid glass and nothing happened.'

'And Karen's face was a picture, when she thought she was going to meet a 90-year-old woman called Edna,' Eileen added. They both laughed. 'But I wonder why Mags went all moody when it looked like there was a message for her. Did she say anything to you when you were washing up?'

'Not much. She doesn't like being called Meg. I don't know why I did that. Well, here we are.' She stopped the car outside Eileen's door. Eileen opened the front passenger door, started to get out, then looked into the back of the car. 'Funny, I thought there was somebody in the car with us,' she said.

'No, who would be? Mags and Karen both go in the opposite direction.'

'No, course there wasn't. Good night then, and thanks for the lift.'

'Good night. See you at Karen's next week, if not before.'

Elspeth turned the corner heading for home. She wished Eileen hadn't said that, about there being someone else in the car. Elspeth could imagine eyes looking at the back of her head, cold shiny blue eyes. She remembered all the horror films she had seen where something terrible appeared in the rear-view mirror. She looked in the mirror anyway. Nothing there, naturally.

She parked outside her block of flats and walked up the path, glad there was no hedge behind which an intruder could lurk, only a low wall with a pair of high gateposts from which the gate had long ago rotted away and never been replaced.

Something was different inside the flat; no cat to meet her. Oscar, her black moggy, always came to the door and rubbed himself against her legs in greeting, before leading the way to the kitchen. Tonight, though, he was not to be seen. Elspeth glanced around the living-room, then went into the bedroom. Oscar was crouching on the bed. When he saw her, he hissed angrily, and leapt on top of her wardrobe. He stood there with the fur standing up on his back, his tail bushed up to three times its normal size, ears flat back on his head, eyes two sparks of lime-green ferocity, and an ugly snarl on his black face. Elspeth had seen him look like that only once before, the previous year, when he had been a kitten and had escaped out of the front door as Elspeth went out to put rubbish in the bin. A passing Rottweiler, who should have been on a lead but wasn't, had menaced him, and he had jumped up on top of the gatepost, standing there looking much as he did now, until Elspeth had rescued him, getting her arms quite badly scratched for her trouble. With Oscar safely inside, she had come out again to shout abuse at the Rottweiler's owner, who had stood by laughing at the incident. He had shouted back and a slanging match had ensued. Neighbours had joined in on both sides, until eventually someone called the police. On the first sight of the flashing blue lights at the end of the street, Elspeth had slipped quietly indoors, while her adversary and his pet legged it around the corner, leaving the neighbours to give confused and conflicting accounts to the police.

Now, Oscar was not to be pacified. He would not come down, even when Elspeth went into the kitchen and noisily scraped Felix from the tin into his bowl. She left it on the kitchen floor, where he would find it when he decided to stop sulking.

Back in the bedroom, Elspeth got undressed, feeling eyes watching her. When she took her underwear off, there was a low snigger, faint but audible. She looked at the window; sometimes Oscar pawed the curtains apart so that he could look out, but tonight they were neatly closed. She had been in all the rooms of the small flat, and there was no place for anyone to hide, certainly not under the bed, which was a divan with only three inches between it and the floor. She was very glad she did not have to bend down and look under it.

Usually, Elspeth made herself a mug of cocoa last thing at night, and watched some television or read a book before going to sleep. Tonight she could not force herself to go back to the kitchen. She knew there was not, could not be, anyone else in the flat, but froze with fear at the thought of passing through the bedroom doorway.

She put on her nightshirt and got into bed, leaving the light on. She heard the snigger again, faintly, but not as if coming from outside, more like someone laughing very softly but very near. Suddenly there was a knock on the bedroom window. Three quick taps, a pause, and one loud rap. She got out of bed and looked out. There was no one there. Back in bed, she heard the same knocking, this time from the kitchen. She did not go to investigate.

Oscar was still on the wardrobe. He was lying down now, with his head on his paws, but his eyes were open. He always slept on Elspeth's bed, but tonight he shunned her.

It seemed useless to try to sleep. She tried to think instead. Fact: Something had taken control of the glass when Elspeth had tried to spell Mags's name. Fact: Eileen had been aware of someone else in the car on the way home, and so had Elspeth, later. Fact: someone – or something – was making noises inside the flat. Conclusion:

Something had followed Elspeth home from Jessica's house.

Elspeth got up and dressed, again feeling those eyes on her body, but at least she was less vulnerable now; she could run out into the night if she had to. She lay on the bed, hearing heavy breathing which was too slow to be Oscar's. Twice more she heard the pattern of four raps, once on the open bedroom door itself. She should have been able to see whoever was knocking, but could not. In the early hours she fell asleep, and woke feeling a weight on her thigh. She hoped to find Oscar's warm furry body; her outstretched fingers touched something cold and damp instead. She sat up in a panic, but there was nothing there.

She lay awake and terrified until the first morning light, when she got up and made herself go into the kitchen. Oscar's food was in the bowl, untouched. From habit, she unlocked the cat-flap in the kitchen door. Instantly Oscar was there, streaking out through the flap. She saw him run straight through the communal back garden, which he shared with two neighbours' cats, and up a tree.

Elspeth had a quick shower – again she felt someone looking at her, but there was no sound this time – and put on clean clothes. She felt unable to face even her usual small weekday breakfast of toast and coffee; there was a heaviness in her stomach which warned her that it would not tolerate the burden of food. She drank some orange juice. It tasted sour and gave her a pain in her throat.

On her way to work, Elspeth realised there was an additional conclusion to be drawn from the facts. Whatever it was had something to do with Mags. She telephoned and arranged to meet Mags for lunch.

'It's such a nice day,' Mags was saying, 'I was just going to get something from the sandwich bar and go to the park.'

'Suits me,' said Elspeth. 'I'll meet you there, by the pond; one o'clock, okay?'

Elspeth felt better at work; she was no longer conscious of the hostile presence. Evidently it couldn't follow her there. Couldn't, or didn't choose to.

The park was bathed in spring sunshine which had attracted some lunch-time workers, but there were a few sparsely populated spots, and Elspeth headed for one of those. It would be easier to talk there than in a crowded café. She had been rehearsing what she would say to Mags; it was going to be difficult to draw her out without seeming to be merely curious.

'Is that all you've brought to eat?' Mags asked, looking at Elspeth's tub of strawberry yoghurt and polystyrene teacup.

'Not very hungry. Had a bad night.'

'Oh, sorry.'

Neither spoke for a few moments, then both spoke at once.

'Is anything wrong?' Mags asked.

'Look, I want to ask you something – I don't want you to think I'm being nosy, but I'd really like it if you'd tell me more about your uncle,' said Elspeth. It had come out all wrong; that wasn't what she had meant to say. If she had to, she would tell Mags everything, about last night and about the way something had taken control of the glass and made it spell 'Meg', but she didn't want to frighten Mags unnecessarily. She remembered how upset Mags had seemed at the time.

Mags was silent for a while, munching her sandwich. At length she said 'Okay. I'd like to talk to somebody about it. I never have, you know. At first I didn't know how to, when I was little, then later it didn't seem to matter. He was my father's brother, Uncle Roger. I don't know if you could call him a paedophile, because he targeted women too, anyone smaller and weaker than himself. He made my life a misery for seven years. It started when I was five, putting his hands where he shouldn't, under my clothes, and saying things to me, and making me do things – touching him –

27

and … I hated him, and I didn't know what to do about it. I couldn't tell my mum or anyone, I didn't know what to say, and I felt dirty and ashamed. I thought I'd be blamed, I really thought it was me doing something wrong. He never actually … you know … raped me. I think now it was because he didn't want there to be any evidence. He must have known my mum would have found out if he did. But he used to tell me about what he did to other children, and I thought, it's only a matter of time before that happens to me. When he visited us I used to run up to my room, but he would come up and knock on the door, I knew it was him because he always knocked the same way, like this …'

Mags rapped on the bench, three quick taps, a pause, and one more. 'And they all thought he was being so nice, sparing the time to come up and chat to the kid. I was the only child, you know. It might not have been so bad if I'd had a sister to share it with. When I got older, about twelve, I understood more what was going on, and I knew it had got to stop. I even thought about telling a teacher at school, but I didn't. And then I found out how to make it stop. One day he was having dinner at our house, and mum had made a mint-chocolate flavoured pudding. He said he wouldn't have any: "I don't eat anything tasting of peppermint."

'Mum said she'd thought he wouldn't mind because it was very mild mint. He said he couldn't take the slightest taste of mint; it made him feel ill just to smell it. So mum opened a tin of fruit salad for him, and as soon as dinner was over I went out and bought lots of Polos and a bottle of peppermint oil. After that, whenever he visited us, I sucked mints, and dabbed the oil on myself like perfume. He was so angry, but there wasn't a thing he could do about it. He kept away from me after that. Mum noticed, of course, but she thought it was just a phase I was going through. I never did tell anyone about it. He died a couple of years later, of a stroke. I don't think the family ever knew what he was really like. You're the only person who knows, and I want it to stay that way.'

28

'Of course, I won't tell anyone. But how could you have kept that to yourself, all that time – surely it must have affected you – I mean …'

'You mean am I terribly traumatised by it all – well no, I'm not, and I think the reason is, I dealt with it by myself. *I* put a stop to it. I didn't tell my parents, or the police, or social workers, or a telephone helpline, I did it all by myself. It made me feel strong and proud, and as if I could cope with anything. I can honestly say it's only had one lasting effect on me – I overdosed on peppermints and now I can't stand them, I never touch the things.'

Elspeth was glad she hadn't told Mags the truth. Mags didn't need to know Uncle Roger was back.

When she arrived home that evening, Elspeth was sucking peppermints and had anointed herself with aromatherapy oil bought from the health food shop.

In the kitchen, she noticed Oscar's food still in the bowl, beginning to smell unpleasant. She emptied it into a plastic bag and put it in the bin, then went into the bathroom. There was a presence there, an air of expectancy, of questioning almost. She took a bag of cotton wool from the cabinet, and pulled off several pieces which she sprinkled with peppermint oil. The presence exploded in rage. She had not been prepared for this. The air around her seemed to blaze with angry threats. Deep inside her she felt a need to appease this fury, to take the mints and the oil and put them outside, open the windows and dispel the aroma, so that the anger would stop.

Instead she took the peppermint-soaked pieces of cotton wool and placed them in each room; kitchen, bathroom, living-room, bedroom, at the back door and the front door, on each windowsill, while all the time the presence battered at her mind. She did not know whether she heard the fearful low-pitched grating sound with her ears or only in her head, but when it stopped, and she heard the beautiful silence, she knew she had won. Uncle Roger had gone back where he came from.

When she got into bed, she was so tired she fell asleep at once, and didn't even wake when Oscar bounced in through the cat-flap and made himself comfortable in the crook of her knees.

IN THE CATACOMBS

Jeffrey Doorn

Dark days and darker nights, that's what I had to face as the war dragged on. Like so many others, I had a loved one at the front; but unlike the women, who could express and share their worries and fears, I had to carry my anxiety bottled up inside. No one knew that Leonard was my lover. Friends, colleagues, even my parents – especially my parents – regarded us as school chums who had remained pals after leaving our studies behind and starting our separate careers.

Those careers could hardly have been more separate. Leonard had taken up a mechanical engineering apprenticeship, while I had pursued librarianship. Still, we managed to find ways to meet and even to be alone together on occasion. Amazing how devious one can become, how adept at subterfuge when forced to conceal one's feelings or mask one's nature. In a perverse way, we actually began to enjoy hiding in the shadows.

However, these brief, infrequent encounters, these stolen moments of pleasure, all came to an end with the war. Leonard was called up, of course, his fit, young body together with his engineering skills making him ideal soldier material. Pacifist though I am, I would almost have relished joining up myself if it meant being near him. Doubtless my unathletic thin build and general lack of strength would have been overlooked; but my weak eyesight, causing me to wear thick spectacles, was sufficient for me to be rejected. Happily, my job in the local library was considered essential work, and I was allowed to keep it.

My co-workers were all women and all older than I; but each had her own unique way of treating me. Dinah, at 24 only three years my senior, regarded me as something of a shirker. Her fiancé was away fighting for his country, so I should be as well, specs or no specs. Susan, unmarried at 40 and in some ways the archetypal spinster librarian (hair in a tight bun, habitually wearing twin set and sensible shoes), had a brother in the army. While we hadn't been particularly close before, once the war had started and her brother was shipped out, she became somewhat friendlier. Perhaps she saw me as something of a surrogate brother; at any rate she took to confiding in me about the odd domestic matter, and kept me posted with news of her soldier. I was often tempted to hint at my own concerns, but thought better of it; though I did wonder if she might have been a lesbian and thus more likely to understand.

The colleague with whom I felt most comfortable and seemed to have the most rapport was, strangely enough, Mabel, Mrs Irwin as I called her until she bade me drop the formality. In her late 50s as far as I could judge, she was certainly older than my mother; yet she had a son about my age, and a daughter a few years older. Both were in the Services, and she was clearly very concerned about their safety, though she never made a fuss about it, as Dinah did about her boyfriend. No, Mabel struck me as the quiet sort of person who might suffer in silence but would never let on. The most she would ever say, when for example she would bring in a piece of cake for me or a home-baked bun, was 'I always make too much; force of habit, I suppose.'

The library was open from 10.00 a.m. to 10.00 p.m. in those days, and I often found myself sharing the evening shift with Mabel. Dinah more often than not contrived to get off early, her evenings apparently being precious to her, despite not having her fiancé around to share them. As for Susan, either looking after her elderly mother or a night out with the girls rendered it inconvenient to work late. I was happy enough to escape the oppressive atmosphere of family meal-times occasionally. And Mabel, being naturally amenable, acknowledged 'It does get a bit lonely, rattling around that great house.'

On one such evening, at about dusk, there was an air raid. There were few readers; after we had ushered them out, Mable watched them scurrying for the safety of the shelter some streets away. 'I don't have the strength to run all that way,' she said. 'You go on ahead; I'll secure the door and go down to the catacombs. It's safe enough there.'

'No, I can't leave you here alone; I'll come down with you.'

'All right, Gil; we'll give each other courage.'

We descended into the vaults, that vast cavernous area beneath the library, used for storage of old furniture, picture frames and the reserve collection of out-of-date or out-of-print material kept for scholarly research or historical completeness. Some of it was ex-catalogue, some spare copies of reference works, some rare and doubtless valuable items, as well as some dross; and while much of it was of limited, esoteric interest, for one reason or another it had been decided to retain, rather than discard, these books. To me, that made them special, intriguing.

As the sounds of the aircraft reverberated above, and the more distant rumble of bombardment began, Mabel moved among the stacks, checking titles and examining the condition of volumes. Perhaps her way of disguising her agitation was to keep moving and make an attempt to keep working. I preferred to sit in a more open area rather than stumble down a dark tunnel or shuffle along the stacks, peering at dusty volumes. Fascinating as they might have been at any other time, they could not hold my attention in my present state. Disturbed by the noise of bombing, my thoughts were of Leonard, wondering what danger he might be in this night. The dim vault, its dark musty corners and mysterious tunnels leading off in several directions, took on an eerie feel, as of the grave. Not for nothing was this underground chamber referred to as the catacombs.

I was staring into the gloom, when I felt a sudden chill. Directly in front of me, emerging it seemed from a tunnel, appeared a wispy figure. Thinking my spectacles had become fogged, I took then off and gave them a quick wipe; but when I replaced them, the figure became more distinct, substantial. It approached, and although my instinct was to call out, I could not utter a sound. It was not Mabel, that was certain, not the porter or anyone else I recognised. The inchoate features had a pallor of death, yet were not frightening. In fact, the closer he came, and it was definitely a man, the calmer I became. He had a kindly look about him, and there was something in his manner and bearing that felt reassuring. A gentle smile formed on his now almost solid face, and he reached out a ghostly hand, making as if to pat me on the shoulder. I sensed rather than heard a message that I shouldn't be afraid, shouldn't worry; that everything would be all right, that I was safe, and that the one I loved was safe. Wanting to know who he was, I tried to reach out; but he slowly shook his head and gave a sad, wistful look, then vanished before my eyes.

Stunned, I did not move a muscle for several minutes. Had what I had just seen been a figment of my imagination or the product of my faulty eyesight? It had seemed so real. Mabel reappeared from beyond the corridor of bookshelves, and I leapt up to tell her of my experience, but then stopped myself. I suppose I felt embarrassed. How could I admit I had seen a ghost? She would think me foolish, and besides, it might upset her. No, I decided, better keep this to myself.

It took me a while to summon the courage to venture down to the vaults again. When I did, there was no sign of anything strange or supernatural; nor did I feel a chill or sense a presence again. As the months went by thoughts of my spooky encounter grew less frequent. There were, to be sure, other things to think about. The war ended, and Leonard came back safe and sound. We resumed our meetings and longed for the day when we could be more open about our relationship. Though we shared our inmost thoughts and told tales of our different experiences, I refrained from divulging my encounter in the vaults.

There were some changes in the library. Dinah left to get married. Susan's mother died shortly after her brother returned, wounded and in need of almost constant attention. Having thus replaced one near-invalid with another, Susan resigned her job to look after him. Mabel was due for retirement, but chose to remain long enough for the new staff to become acclimatised. She also took the lead in mounting an exhibition on the history of the library for the 50th anniversary of its opening.

Being a history buff, I offered to help. The work involved gathering and sifting through photographs, Council minutes, documents and other material from the archives, writing notes and labelling everything carefully, then arranging panels and display cases. One afternoon while thus engaged, Mabel let out a little squeal.

'What is it?' I asked, moving round to the photo-cluttered desk.

'Mr Anstey! Oh sorry Gil, this photograph; it's Esmond Anstey, the Chief Librarian just before I started working here back in the Dark Ages.'

I craned my neck to get a proper look. In a stiff collar and three piece suit with watch chain, a dark-haired man sat on a substantial wooden chair, a formal portrait of a re-spectable gentleman, probably in his early 40s, surrounded by books, the picture of Edwardian propriety. Taking the photograph in my hands, I looked closely at the face and realised with a start that I had seen it before: he was my ghost of the catacombs! Trying not to let Mabel see my astonishment, I quickly asked her to tell me about him.

'Oh, he was said to be ever such a nice gentleman; they all looked up to him. So sad, what happened.'

'What do you mean?'

'Well, it isn't a pretty story. He was ... discovered, caught with a young man, a lad of about your age. They were down in the catacombs. It was a terrible scandal. Mr Anstey was dismissed and publicly disgraced. Then there was the trial; he was imprisoned. After his release he moved to another town. A few years later he died.'

'How did he die?'

'An accident, I think. Can't remember the details, but I believe there was a fire at his place of work. Knowing his reputation, he was probably helping others get to safety: such a thoughtful, selfless man by all accounts. Not that anyone remembered his good qualities at the time of his dismissal. He was shunned until he went to prison, then never spoken of again, except for a few tongue-clucks when news of his death came through. I'm surprised this photograph survived.'

'What shall we do with it?'

'Oh, we'll have to include it in the exhibition. We'll just label it with his name, title and the dates he was here, and leave it at that.'

I returned the photo, biting my lip wondering whether to say anything. No, it might arouse suspicion about my own nature. Mabel looked at the portrait of Esmond Anstey and sighed.

'You know,' she said with a nervous laugh, 'I was too embarrassed to tell you this before, but you remember that night when we sought shelter from the air raid in the catacombs? Well I was standing by a shelf of classical Greek literature when I had the strangest notion I was being watched. I looked up and there before me was a ghost! He seemed to read my thoughts and was trying to tell me something. It wasn't frightening, just startling at first, but I found myself feeling calm, reassured. After he faded away I made my way back to where you were and was going to tell you but suddenly felt silly and dismissed the experience as the product of an overwrought imagination. But now I know the ghost was real – it was Esmond Anstey.

THE OLD COUNTRY

Elsa Wallace

Going to England on holiday would be an education in itself, said Mr Bruce; it didn't matter that Dorrie would miss a few months of school, and she could take her school books with her in any case. The books were packed in the bottom of a trunk and not unpacked until they returned. The journey was leisurely: five days on the train from the Copperbelt to Port Elizabeth; then, as the ship was behind schedule because of engine failure, they boarded her for an unplanned cruise to Lourenço Marques and back. The *Llangibby Castle's* engine faltered again in the Atlantic but the crew seemed used to this; there was no alarm and after a while she chugged on towards the excitement of crossing the line.

They went in the English summer which meant wearing cardigans and saying appreciatively 'It's very fresh' when a cold wind blew. The wonders of early fifties London were overshadowed for Dorrie by the order that when they went home she was not to be friends with Coleen any more. 'She's older than you and it is unhealthy,' said Mrs Bruce. Dorrie knew that Coleen was as healthy as any other girl; and swam ferociously and liked netball. It was surprising she had wanted to be friends. They cycled about, Coleen was teaching Dorrie to do handstands, and they invented stories about the teachers which they wrote in secret books. Perhaps the books had been discovered. The story about Mr Gourlay keeping his deranged mother in a kia at the bottom of his garden might have been going too far. But perhaps it was because of Mrs Kovic. Dorrie had overheard her on the verandah: 'I'm surprised you let your Dorrie play with the O'Leary girl after what happened. I told you she was lying on top of my Lottie – of course Lottie hadn't a clue what was going on.' It was after that that Mrs Bruce had talked to Dorrie in the same uneasy way she had about periods.

'You mustn't take Coleen in your room. Mrs Kovic's brother teaches at a boarding school in the Union, and there the boys aren't allowed to sit on each other's beds.'

'Like in hospital,' said Dorrie, who had often heard nurses scolding visitors off the beds, 'because of the mattress.'

'No,' Mrs Bruce had said impatiently, 'it's nothing to do with the mattress. Because it's unhealthy, or it can lead to that. Anyway, you shouldn't see Coleen so much.'

She had no words to explain what she meant, just as she seemed to have no words for the periods. She had given Dorrie an American booklet to prepare her for the event, but it was vague and disturbing, as it said she might be blue at times. Blue? Then everyone who saw you would know you had this strange thing? As if being skinny, short-sighted and asthmatic weren't enough.

If anyone was unhealthy it was Dorrie herself. The others, all strong and sporty, didn't want to play with her, which was why Coleen's friendship was so special. And now it was to be ended. Unless they could meet secretly behind the anthill at the mine cave-in fence, where you weren't supposed to go. 'We might not go back,' said Mr Bruce before they landed. 'We might stay in England.'

She wondered if she would be allowed to write to Coleen. She would have to write to her to tell her to retrieve the books.

They lodged with Grandma and the aunts in Ealing. Aunt Jean stayed with the Taylors next door to free a bed. Dorrie was struck by how old everyone was. Of course her mother was old. She was forty before Dorrie was born, because, she told her, all the men she might have married had been killed in the first world war, and she had had to emigrate to Africa to marry Dorie's father. Her aunts were older than her mother, and Grandma was 85, a tiny lady who spoke very little and spent most of the day in her room.

It hardly seemed possible that small frail Grandma had produced four large daughters.

Dorrie had rarely seen old people. The population in their mining towns was all young with young families. Once the Smiths had had their parents up from Butterworth and Dorrie had stared at their white hair. Here, age was everywhere; on the streets in the shape of tired women carrying bags of shopping, and at Grandma's house in the photograph albums of dead relatives, some of whom she was hearing about for the first time. Grandpa was but recently dead. When in his teens he had gone to America in a ship with sails but, not prospering, had come to London. A picture showed him hunched in a waistcoat and whittling a toy ship. There were pages of the great-grandparents, great uncles and aunts stiffly posed in formal attire, great-grandmother severe-faced in a brown silk shirt and brocade jacket. These garments of hers were preserved in a mothballed and lavendered trunk, together with green and yellow crinolines, lacy whalebone bodices, and tiny babies' caps minutely tucked.

Her aunts seemed to approve of her, but they thought her vowel sounds odd and Mr Taylor said it was because of the wide open spaces in Africa. She became very conscious of her speech, and even more of what she said. When she told them she liked going to bioscope they exclaimed, 'What do you mean, do you mean lantern slides?'

They were pleased she was quiet, and trusted her to play with the jewellery boxes; there were gold lockets with pictures of her grandparents, high-collared and serious, fragments of gold chains, seals with gold tassels, a tortoiseshell bracelet and comb set with brilliants, silver filigree belt buckles, cairngorm broaches, tiny gold rings set with turquoises and diamonds, jet buttons and beads, a pocket watch with its own little carved wooden stand so that it could be set on a desk. In one box were coral necklaces and earrings, and a long coral wedding garland brought from the South Seas by one of the seafaring great uncles. The most modern things were red lacquer beads and a blue glass amulet, made at the time of the opening of King Tutankhamen's tomb.

What Dorrie liked best were the little tea chests and the writing cases in glossy inlaid wood. The tea boxes were lined with thin tinfoil, and the inner compartments each had a polished well-fitting lid with a tiny bone handle. One stood on little claw feet. The writing cases were even better, gleaming and inlaid with contrasting veneers or strips of brass, and lined with green felt or deep blue velvet. They were flat and neat, or taller and heavy, with inset brass plaques for initials. Pleasant to touch, their contents delighted her; cut glass ink bottles with fitted lids like little hats, sticks of sealing wax, a round black ruler with VR inscribed at one end, dip-in pens with marbled handles, an ornately chased silver cylinder concealing a nib in one end and a propelling pencil in the other. There was a small ivory rod in which was set a tiny lens, and when you looked into this you saw a picture of Alexandra Palace. Her favourite was the heaviest, in black wood. It had lost its nameplate but it had several interior drawers and even a secret drawer. And as if it had produced its own baby it contained, among all the other things, a snuffbox which was a miniature of itself.

Noticing her partiality for it, her grandmother said, 'That belonged to my Uncle Hector, your great-great-uncle. He couldn't take it to Canada with him.' Her voice was a low soft purr and her expression wistful.

Heavy though the box was, Dorrie was to take it back to Africa with her, if they went back. Mr Bruce was having meetings with people and went to Scotland for a few days by himself.

So much in the house was heavy; solid bookcases and deep chairs, formidable wardrobes with bevelled mirrors, so substantial that it was as if they had come from a much larger house. The tea-table was a marvel in itself, having a great shiny sort of mushroom beneath it that you could put your feet on, except that you wouldn't want to scratch the wood.

Dorrie slept in the back bedroom with Aunt May, but she saw little of her, May being at work all day and coming to bed late. The whole house was a novelty to Dorrie: the carpets with creaking wooden floorboards under them, the bathroom, stained glass in the front door, French windows on to the back garden. In later years she couldn't believe it had been anything as mundane as a semi-detached in a row of similar houses. Even the little garden was mysterious with its jasmine and miniature roses, a birdbath shaped like a dolphin, and the air-raid shelter which she longed to explore but which was stuffed with bits of old fencing. She trailed after her parents, sightseeing round museums and the Tower of London, but it was the house that held her interest. Nothing seemed ordinary, not even the glass or china. The large monogrammed cutlery was kept in pockets in a special green felt bag that rolled up, and the pieces were in several patterns, some so old that the flowery initials were nearly worn away. There was a butter knife with a mother-of-pearl handle, sugar tongs, a pierced sugar spoon shaped like a shell, bone china eggcups with birds on the rim, a tea caddy spoon of a pixie on a toadstool.

Grandma seemed like a little ghost in her own house, her fine silky hair in a bun. She always wore a flowered wrapper over her long dark dress, and appeared briefly at meals, eating or drinking very little. On her thin wrist she wore the rolled gold bangle her mother had given her at her wedding, and told Dorrie she should have it one day. Sometimes a small red van stopped in the street and Grandma went out to buy a few groceries; it was the only shopping she did, and it irked Aunt Flora because she could get the things much cheaper elsewhere. Dorrie never asked the questions she wanted to: why was Grandma so small and silent; was she ill, why did people here buy 'seconds' while the good stuff was for export, why were sweets sold in quarters instead of pounds, why was there still rationing, why were the bomb sites still there? So many things puzzled. She was bought a corduroy skirt and slacks. Aunt Jean frowned at them and said, 'I don't think they're quite you.' Dorrie couldn't fathom what she meant. Clothes were bought for you and you wore them, that was all.

One day Mr Bruce came home in a temper. They were not staying he said; he had had enough of the old country, the traffic fumes in Oxford Street, not to mention the poppycock he had to put up with from some people. They were booked to return on the *Edinburgh Castle*.

Mrs Bruce acquiesced, saying she had forgotten how cold England was. She sorted through photographs with her sisters to choose some for herself, some of the old family up north but chiefly of the four sisters on their jolly camping holidays in the West Country, or in Belgium and France. It was a dull day and Dorrie, having frightened herself looking at some cigarette cards of Raemaker's War Cartoons, was watching television. This was supposed to be a great treat, but it was nothing as good as Tom Mix or Margaret O'Brien or Wild Bill Hickock, whom both she and Coleen liked and would imitate, pretending their bikes were horses.

On the little grey screen a man with a goatee beard sang 'Heigh-ho, heigh-ho, it's summer time in Fontainbleau.' Dorrie began leafing through magazines, half listening to her mother and aunts.

'There are none of *him*, I suppose,' Mrs Bruce was saying.

No, nothing much from that side. These are all Dad's people. Here's Grandpa; doesn't he look a tartar.'

Dorrie had seen the wedding pictures of Grandma's parents, both as grim as if they had just received very bad news.

Mrs Bruce said, 'Great-Uncle John – now he went to Auckland, didn't he and he came back with that awful Limehouse girl. Hector never did come back, did he?'

42

'Of course not,' said Aunt Jean firmly. 'He *had* to leave.'

'Bancruptcy, was it?'

'NO!' scoffed Jean. 'A touch of the Oscar Wildes At *that* time, you know.'

'Oh.' Mrs Bruce nodded and glanced round at Dorrie who pretended to be fascinated by the miniature of Roley Robin's life. 'Of course, he left in a hurry.'

'It's a shame really,' said Aunt May. 'Though he did pretty well for himself in Canada; he was Governor of one of the Provinces eventually. Mother always says he was her favourite uncle. She says he had the most beautiful scented handkerchiefs.'

'He still has, according to her,' put in Aunt Flora. 'If she's to be believed, he does come back, handkerchiefs and all.'

'Oh that's all havers,' Jean said firmly. 'She hardly knows when she's dreaming or not these days.'

Dorrie was taking handkerchiefs home for Coleen, an unimaginative present but they were all she had. Her mother had bought them for her in Las Palmas, but she would give them to Coleen. She had wanted to buy her a picture frame in Woolworths, but Mrs Bruce wanted to know what it was for and she couldn't think of a convincing reply quickly enough. She could have said it was for a picture of Grandma. Perhaps she could give Coleen one of the glass bottles from Great-Uncle Hector's writing case. Perhaps no one would notice.

The box stood on the chest of drawers beside her bed. It was to be put into her trunk at the last to crush down the new clothes. Next to it was another box, long and slim, of blond wood painted with ferns. It contained the narrow tan elbow gloves that had belonged to Great-Aunt Clara. They were so shrunk now that they would fit no one. There was a pair of silver glove-stretchers and because Dorrie had admired the patterns on them she was to have them as well.

'Because you're our favourite niece,' said Aunt Jean.

'But I'm your only niece.'

'That's what we mean,' said Aunt Flora.

Dorrie was packed off to bed early on her last night, even though it was still light. She lay awake watching the wallpaper, another novelty, and just aware of the murmurs downstairs. The mattress was domed and lumpy. She had slid right off the bed the first night and Aunt May had exclaimed. She thought about the narrow comfort of the cabin bunk and how she would soon be speeding across the green Atlantic, with a stop perhaps at Madeira.

She could buy Coleen something in Madeira if she had the right money. Would Coleen still be on the Roan when they got back? Her father, like Dorrie's, seemed to want to be on the move; they had been to Nairobi, Fort Rosebery, Shabani, even Windhoek. She had no photograph of Coleen. The only keepsake would be the notebooks, if they were safe in the tin in the garage, and the perfectly round milky quartz pebble Coleen had given her in the bush near the tailings dump. All the grass there had been burned, and Coleen prised the stone from the blackened earth. There had been the smell of grass fires that day and after a while tiny black leaves came drifting down. She tried to recall the heat of the afternoon, the clicking noise the grasshoppers made, the sky's white-blue, Coleen in her yellow cotton frock, her black plaits swinging over her shoulders, her dark eyes. Coleen sang and whistled 'Oh my darling Clementine' and once she changed it to 'Oh my darling Dorrie-tine' and they had both laughed to falling down, and Dorrie was filled with happiness.

'You'll make other friends.' Mrs Bruce had said abruptly when Dorrie had dared to protest about the ban. But she had no idea how hard it was to gain a friend, in that school, where everyone was so fit and sports-mad; how conspicuously alone, when no one wanted you. And but for Coleen no one did.

Mrs Bruce had liked her once – 'You want to learn to speak like Coleen, she speaks beautifully.' And now there might be no more days like that day in the bush, being given the pebble hot from the sun, hot from Coleen's hand. It was a beautiful thing the size of a hen's egg. How generous of Coleen to give it to her. If she had found it herself, would she have given it up? The dried grass stalks had crunched under their feet. New green shoots were needling up through the scorched earth. She breathed in the smell of the distant fire, such a characteristic smell. But it was overlaid with something now. Something fresh and sweet, like vanilla, like cologne and with a sharpness like lemon to it.

She opened her eyes to see someone lightly crossing the room. It should have been Aunt May, but was as tall as her father. It was not her father; he would have made a noise, or would have been exaggeratedly cautious not to wake her. This person's step was swift and easy. She gasped and held her breath. The figure stooped over Great-Uncle Hector's box, and then turned and smiled at her.

It was all over in a moment; the soundless crossing of the room, the hand touching the box, a fall of dark hair over a white forehead, the turned head, a quick slant of a smile and then he was gone. The net curtains stirred a little, as if breathing the delicious scent still lying over her in the quiet air.

SMOKE

Martin Foreman

Friday. Half past seven on an autumn evening. A bar in the city, one of a chain, pine floors, Irish script and bar staff in white and black.

Words and laughter echoing, multiplying, ricocheting.

Couples and groups, mostly white, young and employed. Clothing from quiet to fashionable, accents from gentle to anonymous.

Men and women lean towards each other, eyes locked in conspiracy and lust. Nearby, friends and workmates get drunk, mock bosses, judge popstars and sportsmen. Pauses are few. Into any void questions are thrown: what to do now, where to go, what to eat. Drinks pass from hand to hand, bottles and glasses are emptied. Cigarettes burn slowly. Smoke wafts in the air.

At a table by the window chairs and benches are pushed back, coats pulled on and bags collected. The conversation moves towards the door and into the night.

Around the table silence gathers. A waiter, twenty-four, Mediterranean, blue-eyed and dark-haired, with an undeclared admirer at the bar and broken hearts all over town, removes stained glasses and crumpled crisp packets. A half-full cigarette pack remains. Returning with a clean ashtray, he wipes the table, picks up the pack, looks round, sees no claimant, drops it back onto the glistening surface and returns to anonymity.

The chairs and benches slumber.

The table, ashtray and cigarettes wait.

The door opens. Three men, three women, all in their twenties. Four settle at the table, two offer drinks.

Names emerge, attach themselves to faces and body language. Duncan is short, scruffy-haired and almost handsome, with an irreverent sense of humour. Ellen is

46

petite, blond, pretty, uncertain. Tom is tall, sharp-featured and piercing-eyed, a should-be model wondering which of the women will be his for the evening. Shona, in the armchair, the oldest, close to thirty, is statuesque and calm, a welcoming port in any storm, still waters running deep. Rick, returning from the bar with designer lager, vodka and stimulant, is the intelligent gay man recently separated from his lover, but beginning to think life is worth living again. Clara, bringing the last of the drinks, tired at the end of a long day, is the cynic.

'Thank God for this.' 'Cheers.' 'Ta.' Glasses raised, smiles shared.

Conversation restarts. 'I've had a hell of a week.' Clara.

Expressions commiserate at orders not delivered, phone calls not answered, burdens that no one should have to bear. Shona rummages in her bag, puts it down disappointed. With relief she reaches for the cigarette pack, waves it in the air. 'Anybody's?'

'No.' Heads shaken. 'No.'

'I thought you'd given up.' Rick.

'I had.' She offers the pack round. No takers. The cigarette at her lips, she finds a lighter, flicks the flame into life and inhales.

The first cigarette she smoked, at a friend's house at thirteen, an exercise in adulthood, hit her with the impact of a lorry smashing into a wall. The most recent, puffed in the street an hour ago, had no more taste than water. This one has the scent of Araby, the sparkle of champagne, the mist of distant moors. She looks at the packet. A brand she does not know.

'My great-aunt died of lung cancer.' Duncan.

'You don't seem too upset about it.' Ellen.

'She left me money.'

'I have no intention of dying or leaving you any money.' Shona smiles.

Duncan grins back. 'Don't need it.'

47

'It's a filthy habit.' Tom's beauty allows him latitude that women grant to few men. 'Your breath stinks, your clothes stink … '

'Which is why God invented chewing-gum and washing-machines.' Duncan.

'Cigarettes can be sexy.' Rick. 'Bette Davis, Marlborough Man.'

'Lung cancer. Emphysema.' Clara.

'Everything's bad for you.' Ellen. 'Even drink.'

'I once had a cousin who drank forty Benson and Hedges a day.' Duncan.

The conversation swirls as slowly as smoke, dissolving into some sport and the national team. Tom fascinates Ellen with a comparison of the merits of watching games live or on television. Rick, Duncan and Clara move on to film and Hollywood stars. Shona sits in the middle, watching, listening.

You're a fool, she thinks, watching Ellen teeter between hesitation and eagerness. He can't take his eyes off you, but in forty-eight hours you'll be an embarrassment. It will be six weeks before you realise he never offered more than sex, and six months before it hits you how he used you.

She met her own Tom at sixteen. Sitting in a bar with low lighting and high pretensions, only the cigarette and the studied calm with which she occasionally puffed it masked her nerves and embarrassment. 'You're cool,' said a youth two years older as he stared into her eyes, and coolly she inhaled and coolly she let the smoke dribble from her nostrils. Later that night she ignored the pain with which he took her virginity, but in the days that followed she howled in agony when he ignored her phone calls. It was the tobacco which saved her, transforming her regret into anger and anger into contempt. Over the years that contempt subsided and now she is no longer sure which emotion, if any, remains.

She turns to the others. It should be Duncan, she silently tells Rick, you look good together and you're both

48

dependable and fun. But it would never occur to Duncan to dabble on the far side of the blanket. And Clara, my dear, while you might yet strike lucky, you will not do so here. Complain about the world too much and the world will turn a deaf ear.

Another breath. The smoke clears her senses and she looks across the bar, seeing each figure in sharp relief. Clothes melt away, revealing bodies tanned and well-toned or flesh pale and sagging, upright posture or stooping backs predicting failure of tendon and cartilage. Each smoker stands out, lit not by the flame of tobacco but the dull fire of their hearts, sending waves of light through arteries and capillaries to give each skin a warm, insubstantial glow.

That was how she used to feel. As her friends drowned the sweat of aerobics with the scents of the Body Shop, she sat calmly in upmarket bars sipping the latest cocktail, smoking the slimmest cigarettes and entranced by the egos of men half a generation older. Some she let seduce her, from curiosity more than desire. And if she returned home alone, at the end of the night there was always the last cigarette to satisfy at least one of her cravings without the complication of forced conversation or misplaced passion.

She drinks her beer, smiles at Tom and Ellen's increasing intimacy. Tom's telephone rings. He pulls it out, frowns at the number, answers it stuttering like a little boy discovered doing wrong. Another girl, a date he has forgotten, an old flame, a casual encounter that he has yet to conquer. He has not yet mastered the art of lying to one woman in the presence of another. Ellen stares into space, forcing herself not to listen to what she can hear.

Across the table, Duncan is telling the tale of an embarrassing dinner with an MP. At the punchline, Shona laughs and they turn to her, surprised.

'Another drink, anyone?' Duncan, standing up. 'Ask now or forever hold thy peace.'

49

Orders are given. Shona looks at her glass, decides not, stubs out her butt, unaware that her right hand is already reaching for the one to follow.

'How's your love life?' Rick to Clara.

'Non-existent.'

'Like mine,' Shona adds, and politeness descends as if she were an uninvited guest. What am I missing? she wonders as she embarks on the story of the last man she had hopes of, a Canadian engineer with a mental illness as predictable as showers on a spring day.

The story ends with the common refrain – 'it's about time I met someone decent'. Relieved, the others return to each other. Now she understands. She has let her defences down. This is not the Shona they know, nor the Shona she imagines herself to be. 'Now, wait a second, guys,' she wants to say, but she does not do petulant. Instead, she drains the last of her vodka and pulls hard at the half-finished cigarette, inhales lust and longing, romance and regret.

She sits back in her chair, suddenly bored. Looking round the bar again, she notices without noticing who has moved and who has stayed in the same position, who is coming in and where they will sit or stand. The smokers are as distinct as before, only this time it is not their beating hearts and their flowing blood that she sees, but their skeletons, solid, dull and grey, portraits of a death to come. She is less shocked than surprised, overwhelmed by an emotion that lies somewhere between the shiver of fear and the warmth of affection.

Then the vision clears and for a moment she is tempted to seek their companionship, to stand up, go and speak to each of them in turn, listen to their stories, laugh or commiserate. But she has no energy and she turns back to those around her, to Duncan returning and the bounty he brings. With every word they utter and gesture they make, they become more distant, as if they are strangers or have met in a dream. No, it is more mundane than that. She is getting old, and it is not friends she wants, but a lover, a husband, although the word still frightens with its suggestion of finality and fidelity until death.

Another stub extinguished, another fag lit. At least a dozen still wait in the packet, lined up like men sharing a bed. Life should be so simple. Choose a partner, settle down, when he has turned to ash, return to the store for the identical model, or one beefier, taller or less demanding. Stop when you get bored. Start again when the impulse takes you.

Not long ago there almost was a husband, a man who shared her bed and politics, her taste in music and cigarettes. But over the year they were together she grew bored, as he resisted adulthood and she yearned to grow old. When they separated she gave up smoking, as if it had been he, not the tobacco, that was the addiction.

Three weeks ago she realised her twenties were about to leave her forever, the faint cracks that had appeared in a once perfect smile had come to stay. At the end of an evening when she had drunk one glass too many, when the man she had thought unattached had called an unnamed partner to say he was coming home, when she could not find a taxi and rain had begun to fall, she had walked into an off-licence for shelter and walked out with twenty Dunhill. The first one calmed her, the second was an old friend. The third she could not remember. The fourth and fifth brought back memory, the sixth and seventh excitement. Cigarettes gave her life, cigarettes gave her life meaning. Without cigarettes she might as well die.

She comes back to the present as if a lifetime has passed. Ellen and Tom are so close as to be ready to leave. They will sit for an hour in one of the restaurants nearby where couples cocoon themselves in candlelight and wine. Afterwards, perhaps, they will go to a nightclub, although Tom is too impatient to dance and all Ellen wants is to hold him at night and wake up in the morning and forgive him his stubble and bad breath. Sex she does not think about, afraid that when it comes it will be less bonus than drawback.

The smoke settles against the walls of Shona's lungs as gently as a feather wafting onto snow, seeps into her bloodstream as sweetly as honey and drifts idly onwards as a slow-moving stream on a summer's day. She is floating, at peace, detached from the world.

There is laughter on her right. Clara, grasping Duncan's arm as she giggles. It means nothing. It should be Ellen at Duncan's side and Clara about to leave with Tom. Duncan would never disappoint Ellen and Clara would have no illusions about Tom's intentions. She would take him home, pull him onto her and kick him out in the morning. Two days later he would wonder why she did not return his calls. If they could each get beyond the other's armour, they might be good for each other. She would ground him; with his wings clipped, he would mature, become, to his own surprise, a devoted husband and father.

As for Rick … He has the combination of wit, humour and intelligence that she seeks. Perhaps if they went out together, she might work a miracle, persuade him of the virtues of vagina and breasts. If all else fails, she can be the classic fag hag until he finds his Mr Right. The classic fag hag even after he has found him.

'Go on to a club afterwards, shall we, Rick?' she says, her voice a mock seductive whisper. Rick does not hear. She will ask again when they leave and if he has other plans make her way home. With thirty channels of television and a bottle of vodka her options are open.

Across the bar the scene has shifted again. People are more relaxed. Hands and bodies are closer, opinions louder and only occasionally offensive. The staff move quickly and efficiently, enjoying the buzz, looking forward to the tips at the end of the evening. A group of smokers in a corner hands round cigarettes like sweets among children. Their shapes shift, revealing not skin and skeletons but buried spots and stains, tumours and ulcers. Some are barely visible, others are large and bright. All cling to their hosts like limpets, enveloping organs and sinews. One or two twitch, grow imperceptibly. She looks up, but the faces reveal nothing, laugh and talk unaware of the parasites within.

Fascinated, she takes a long draught of smoke that for a moment clears her vision. 'Do you see that?' she asks the others, but they pay no attention. 'Do you see that?' she repeats, louder, but she can hardly hear her own voice. Suddenly, panic seizes her. What if she is harbouring one of these creatures, what if the cancer is already eating her away? What if her future has already been destroyed, if death really lurks in the cigarette she holds?

Across the table, half a lifetime away, is a man she once knew. 'Rick!' she shouts, but the word is silent. Her glance falls. Her clothes have fallen away, her hands, her arms, her body are ghostly grey. As she stares at the flesh, it begins to dissolve, become almost transparent. Only the half-smoked cigarette is real, floating up in a half-formed hand to rest on insubstantial lips.

She is desperate to speak, but her mouth, her jaw, are numb. Beside her, Tom and Ellen have stood up and he is helping her with her coat. Rick and the others get up. They speak to each other but Shona hears nothing. 'Hey,' she tries to call as they walk away, but her lungs are motionless. She is not breathing, she cannot breathe, breath is no longer necessary.

'Hey,' she tries again, 'wait for me.' She would stand but she has no legs, push herself up but she has no arms, move but has no body, think but has no …

On the threshold, Clara looks back to check they have left nothing, but only empty glasses, a half-filled ashtray and open cigarette packet remain. As the door closes behind her, a cloud of smoke hovering over the table drifts apart. A waitress comes over, collects the glassware. The pack she leaves for someone else to pick up.

OLD HAUNTS

Alice Windsor

'Let's face it, Patrick,' said Richard. 'It isn't working, is it?'

'I suppose not,' Patrick replied slowly, 'but I'm not ready to give up yet. Not without a fight.'

'That's just it,' said Richard. 'Fight is about all we do these days.'

'I didn't mean fight with you, you know that. I meant fight whatever it is that's gone wrong.'

Things had certainly gone wrong between them. When they had met the summer before last, on holiday in Southend, they had both felt an instant attraction that had soon developed into a feeling of total compatibility. Not that they always agreed about everything, but they were able to disagree without resentment. Each could bring to the other new ideas, new ways of looking at things, so that their discussions were always lively, and they were never bored with each other. So compatible were they that after a few months each felt he wanted, more than anything in the world, to spend the rest of his life – or at least the foreseeable future – with the other. At 28 and 29, they considered themselves old enough, and experienced enough, to trust their own judgement. Quite simply, they loved each other, in a way that was something new for them both.

It had seemed the obvious and natural thing to set up home together, and both being established in their careers (Richard was the youngest solicitor in his firm, and Patrick taught English to immigrants) they decided to buy a house jointly. House-hunting proved to be one of the most enjoyable enterprises in which they had ever engaged. They looked at dozens of houses and flats; the purpose-built flats and warehouse conversions that Richard liked Patrick considered lacking in character, while the Victorian terraced houses that appealed to Patrick were, according to Richard, located in scruffy areas where the neighbours would soon suss out that they were gay and react adversely. They didn't care. They were enjoying the search, and having no property to sell, were in no hurry to buy.

This pleasant state of affairs was coming to an end – Richard, observing an ominous steep rise in property prices, had begun to wonder how far their finances could stretch – when they found what appeared to be the perfect solution. The small terraced house, although in dilapidated condition, preserved enough of its original features to please Patrick, while Richard claimed that his observations of the state of the neighbours' tiny front gardens, and the make and condition of the cars parked outside, convinced him that this was an up and coming area where the locals would not care that Richard and Patrick were a couple, if they even bothered to notice.

The house would need money spent on it, to make it into the sort of home they wanted. Patrick took on extra work coaching children for their GCSE and A-level exams, mostly the sons of ambitious families who were ambitious for their daughters too, but not to the extent of allowing one-to-one sessions with a male teacher. One bearded bigot all but spelled it out: 'Of course, we must find a lady tutor for the girls, you understand,' he had said with an all-men-together, no-offence-intended smile. *I understand,* Patrick thought. *It's you who don't. If you only knew.* As it happened, their sons were as safe in his hands as their daughters would have been; he might allow his eyes to delight in a handsome face, but that was as far as it went. Patrick was a monogamist.

Richard obtained a mortgage on what he said were the most favourable terms possible. Contracts were exchanged, and at last the day came when they received the keys. They stood in the kitchen discussing the changes they would make. The pantry door would be removed, and a big window put in the back wall, to give more light and a view of the back garden. Patrick muttered something about an RSJ, and Richard said they were paying a builder to worry about that sort of thing. The back garden was shoulder-deep in abundantly-flowering, thorny, deep red roses, together with a profusion of prickly thistles, brambles and nettles. Richard decided the roses could stay; he would prune, feed and water them till they reached perfection. The rest would go. Richard would undertake the garden work himself; Patrick was too soft-hearted and would want to leave patches of nettles for the butterflies.

Upstairs, the smallest of the three bedrooms would become a bathroom. In the largest bedroom, which overlooked the back garden, Patrick exclaimed with renewed pleasure at the fireplace with its original art nouveau tiles, while Richard, looking out of the window, observed with satisfaction the smart new conservatories and kitchen extensions which most of their neighbours had built. What remained of those back gardens were tidy lawns, a few shrubs, the odd flowerbed. How pleased the neighbours would be when Richard took his garden in hand and stopped it producing weed seeds to pollute the tamed backyards around.

It was while they were thus pleasantly occupied that the first shadow of desolation touched them. Richard felt a sense of helpless misery and, without speaking, hurried out of the room and downstairs to escape it, but in vain. The weight of despair followed him, and he stood in the kitchen aghast. In the bedroom, Patrick felt suffocated. He opened a window, but found no relief. Dread lay in the depth of his body, as if he had an appointment for some long and painful dental work.

That was the start. Neither again felt comfortable in the new house. They moved in, living with bits of old furniture donated by and borrowed from friends and relatives, to avoid continuing to pay rent on their furnished flat. They had even looked forward to the period of rough living while they waited for the house to take shape, but it proved much rougher than they had expected. The workmen they employed to transform it into their ideal home turned out to be surly and inefficient; the work went slowly, and they lived surrounded by rubble. Lacking cooking facilities, they ate corn flakes, sandwiches and takeaways, but found they had little appetite for them. They argued constantly; not the lively discussions they had enjoyed before, but petty squabbles over small domestic upsets that built up into towering rages on Richard's part, and lengthy impenetrable sulks on Patrick's. Since moving in, they had not been to bed except to sleep, and they slept badly, disturbed by dreams.

One night Patrick awoke to find himself sitting up in bed, holding a pencil, a book on his knees. He had written in the margin 'Why dont you go back were you come from you poffs. Your not wanted here.'

'How can we fight whatever it is, we don't *know* what it is,' said Richard. 'All I know is we were happy before and now we aren't. One of us will have to go, that's all. You can't keep up the mortgage on your own, and I can. So ...'

Patrick did not point out that, were they to split up, Richard would owe him his half of the deposit; that would only send him into one of his rages. Instead he said quietly 'Couldn't we at least try to get some help first? What about the girls, they might help.'

'Girls? What girls? You mean Iris and Sylvia? How could they help?'

'I just thought ... they have that bookshop ... they might have picked up some ideas ...'

'From the bookshop? You mean you really think this place is ... no, Patrick, not even you could be that daft.'

Patrick showed him the book. 'I wrote this in my sleep one night last week.'

'I never knew you were so self-oppressed,' said Richard.

'Self-oppressed? *Me!*'

'You must be, to have written that.'

'That's the point. I didn't write it.'

'You just said you did.'

'My *hand* wrote it. *I* didn't. Don't you see, there's something in this house that doesn't want us here. It's trying to drive us out. I think we should see if we can't drive it out instead.'

'You're mad. Your unconscious mind wrote that, because you're ashamed of who you are.'

Patrick refrained from pointing out that Richard was the one who had rejected several excellent houses because he thought he detected potential homophobia among the neighbours. 'Even unconsciously, I wouldn't use such grammar and spelling,' he said. 'I am an English teacher. *Please*, Richard, just give it a try. What have we got to lose?'

'Our reputations as sane people?' Richard suggested.

But in the end he agreed to see the 'girls'; Iris and Sylvia had invited them to supper anyway, so if Patrick wanted to raise the matter Richard would not object. He did not tell Patrick about the old man he had seen on several occasions, standing at the foot of their bed in the dark, radiating hostility. That was, of course, just a recurring bad dream.

Sylvia owned a shop in a side street off the High Road. It had been in her family for generations when it was a pawnbroker and second-hand jeweller, but to the family's disgust Sylvia had decided to turn it into a bookshop specialising in the supernatural, branching into horror and science-fiction. 'SPOOKY BOOKS' had been painted over the shop front, and the three brass balls taken down.

The family had begged Sylvia's father to make her see sense, but he, on inheriting the shop, had signed it over to Sylvia to do with as she saw fit. He had no interest in running any kind of shop, being absorbed in his career as an air traffic controller at Gatwick. Sylvia knew perfectly well that she could not make a profit, or even a living, out of such a shop in such a district, but it provided free accommodation, while her girlfriend Iris's job paid the bills.

Iris taught painting, pottery and flower-arranging to pensioners and housewives at the same college where Patrick taught English. They had become staff-room friends there, and before long had introduced each other to their respective partners. Richard, being Richard, was quick to find an advantage. Lively attractive Sylvia made an ideal escort for office socialising, entertaining important clients, even the odd visit to his parents. She, for her part, had a liking for dressing up and consuming expensive food and drink, tastes which could seldom be indulged on Iris's salary.

'You're Richard's beard,' Iris commented on one such occasion, watching Sylvia applying eyeliner with an unaccustomed but deft hand.

'I'm his *what?*'

'A woman who goes around with a gay man so that he can pretend to be straight is known as his beard,' Iris explained.

'I don't know where you pick up such expressions,' Sylvia complained. 'Must be these pensioners you mix with at work.'

Now, minus eyeliner and wearing a simple yellow shift dress, Sylvia was ladling leek and potato soup into ivy-leaf-patterned bowls.

Patrick had intended to raise the subject of the haunted house when they reached the pudding and coffee stage, but suddenly felt he could wait no longer, and while Richard raised his eyes heavenward to demonstrate his detachment, Patrick explained their predicament.

'So we were wondering if you could maybe help us in any way,' he ended.

Iris and Sylvia looked at each other.

'No,' said Sylvia, 'but we know a man who can. Probably.'

'He has a very good success rate,' said Iris.

'And he's one of us,' said Sylvia.

'He won't charge you much,' said Iris.

'He won't charge you anything,' said Sylvia. 'He owes us a favour or two, and we'd be glad to call them in on your behalf. Now, when can he come to assess the situation?'

'Sooner the better, sounds like,' said Iris.

And while the soup cooled in the bowls, Sylvia telephoned Silas and arranged for him to call on Patrick and Richard the following Sunday evening.

'Oh yes,' said Silas, standing in the hallway. 'You have something here. But it is so unhappy. Angry, resentful - *he* is. It's a man, an old man. And he is here in the present.'

They looked at him, Richard sceptically, Patrick hopeful and questioning.

'By that I mean he isn't any kind of re-play. Let me explain: some hauntings are re-enactments of past events, like recordings being played back. There is no consciousness there, any more than William Shatner is personally present when you play a video of *Star Trek*. But what you have here is a conscious being, aware of himself, his surroundings and you.'

'Can he do us any harm?' asked Patrick.

'Hasn't he already? Isn't that why I'm here?' Silas asked.

'I meant, any physical harm?'

'Probably not. I couldn't guarantee it. Do you ever feel inexplicably cold, in a warm room for instance? Well, that's when he is taking energy from his surroundings and from you. He can use that energy to move small objects – place something for you to trip over, or switch lights off and on. Have you experienced anything like that?'

They nodded, Patrick eagerly, Richard grudgingly.

'But who is he?' Patrick asked. 'Did he live here once? How did he die?'

'Yes, he lived here for a long time. I can't see how he died. This is unusual. Normally, their deaths are important to them, they are in the forefront of – oh, this is *most* interesting. I have heard of this, of course, but I never encountered one before ...'

'One *what*?'

'He isn't dead. His body is alive, somewhere, and he has become detached from it. He didn't want to leave here; he loved this house, he still loves it, and he resents your presence here. You are trespassers in his view, and he dislikes you because you are gay. He dislikes me because I am black. He wants us all out of his house.'

'But we can't – what can we do?' Richard asked.

'As I said, I have not encountered one of these before. I shall study the matter further. In the meantime, the best suggestion I can make is that you try to locate this man's body – it could be that if you bring them together – his name is George, by the way, I can't get his surname.'

'Well, that was a fat lot of help,' Richard grumbled after Silas had left.

'Don't be so negative,' said Patrick; 'he's given us something to go on. We have to find this George and try to reason with him. See the people we bought the house from, that will be a start.'

The previous owner was a property company, MacGregor and Melville, which had formerly owned and rented out streets of houses in the district, but several years before had decided to get out of the renting business, selling off their houses as they became vacant, and speeding up the process by offering generous discounts to sitting tenants who wished to buy their homes. The young man at the local office had at first been reluctant to divulge information about the last tenant of Richard and Patrick's house, but Richard produced his business card and spun a yarn about a client who had swindled George out of some money many years before and who now, believing himself to have little time to live, wished to make restitution.

'Well – I suppose there's no harm –' said the young man, 'George Turner was one of the stubborn ones. He couldn't or wouldn't find the money to buy his place, even though we were offering it at half the market rate, just to get it off our hands. He was too old to get a mortgage if he'd wanted one, so we were resigned to keeping him on till he died; then one day his son turned up, said the old man had become incapable of looking after himself – falling down and not being able to get up, turning the gas on and forgetting to light it, leaving the taps running and flooding the place, the usual stuff. He was putting him in a home, the son said, and gave us the keys. That's the last we heard of him.'

'Could you possibly tell us which home?'

After a brief rummage in a file the young man came up with 'Shady Sycamores, in Forest Gate.'

'No, love, nobody that name here,' said the fat woman at Shady Sycamores.

'Are you sure?' asked Richard, and began to trot out his story – solicitor – client – money.

'Wait a minute,' called a skinny woman at the desk. 'George Turner, wasn't that the old bloke who was only with us a couple of days? The one we had to send to Lamburne Street? Year before last?'

'Think you're right,' said the fat woman. 'You see,' she explained to Richard, 'we can't keep them here unless they can feed themselves, wash themselves, take themselves to the toilet. We can't do all that for them, we're not a nursing home. We either have to send them to a proper nursing home, if they got the money, or Lamburne Street Hospital, if they've not. Oh, that Lamburne Street; I pray I never end up in that place.'

Lamburne Street Hospital's exterior was indeed grim with a hundred and fifty years of accumulated human misery, but inside a cheerful young nurse readily directed Richard and Patrick to the ward where George Turner's body sat in an armchair.

'He's usually out in the garden,' she explained, 'but it's too wet today. He doesn't understand, of course, it's all the same to him where he is, but I like them to get the fresh air and sunshine when they can. You his sons?'

Richard started on his tale about the swindling client.

'That won't mean anything to George,' said the nurse, 'but you can tell his daughter. She comes to visit him every Tuesday morning. I'll leave you now, stay as long as you like.'

'Hello, George,' said Patrick. George stared at him, and for the first time Patrick fully understood the saying, 'The lights are on but there's nobody home.' George's eyes were alive, but there was nobody there. They were windows of an empty room.

The nurse left the ward.

'Stand up, George,' said Patrick.

George stood up.

'Would you like to go outside?' asked Patrick.

George made no reply.

'Walk over to the window,' said Patrick. George did so.

'Now come back to your chair and sit down,' said Patrick. George obeyed.

'What's all that about?' asked Richard.

'Just trying something,' Patrick answered. 'He seems to be able to hear and understand me speaking to him, but he's got no mind of his own, he can't refuse to do what I tell him. It's as if his mind is elsewhere.'

'Yes, it's at our house, giving us a hard time,' said Richard, whose scepticism seemed to have dissolved.

'We should come back tomorrow, when his daughter's here,' said Patrick.

'Poor Dad,' said June, 'I blame Derek – that's my brother. Dad wasn't so bad; he couldn't look after himself, that's true, but he had his faculties, he wasn't a vegetable like what he is now. It was Derek forcing him to leave his house that done it. Dad loved that house. He was born there, you know. From the very day Derek drove him to Shady Sycamores, he went right down; he couldn't even stay at the Sycamores, that's how he ended up in this dump.'

'Yes, the nurse told us,' said Patrick.

'Well, I'd have had him to live with me, like a shot, but my husband wouldn't have it. They never got on, you see. I argued and argued, but he wouldn't budge. Now I'm a widow, I can do what I want, but it's too late for poor Dad. You see what he's like. I couldn't cope with him, not the way he is.'

'But if he was to get better,' Patrick said cautiously. 'Suppose he went back to how he was before he left his house ...'

'Oh, I'd have him with me then, course I would. But it's not going to happen, is it?'

'I still think we should take June into our confidence,' said Patrick.

'Don't be ridiculous,' Richard said. 'She'd think we were mad, she wouldn't trust us, we wouldn't be let near George ever again. We'd lose what chance we have of putting things right. No, we've got to do this ourselves. Present her with the *fait accompli*. She'll thank us for it afterwards.'

It took some organising. Silas was waiting at the house. Sylvia was on her way to Loughton in her van, to fetch June, Richard having ascertained that June would be at home. The weather, on which the plan depended, was obligingly fine. Richard was in his car in the hospital car park. Patrick strode, with a misleading air of confidence, into the garden. A nurse was looking at him. He gave a cheery wave, and called 'Just going to visit old George.' The nurse smiled and nodded, and went on pushing an old man in a wheelchair up the ramp.

Patrick located George, sitting on a bench beside a fish pond. He wasn't looking at the fish. He wasn't looking at anything. Using his technique of simple direct orders, Patrick got him to walk over to the shrubs that bordered the garden. The next bit would be tricky. It was impossible to convey to George the need for stealth, but he managed to keep them both behind the cover of the bushes until they reached the gate that led from the garden to the car park. The gate was closed but not locked, and it squeaked as Patrick opened it. There was nobody about in that part of the garden, but there were people coming and going in the car park, staff and visitors. This was it. Until now, Patrick could have claimed to be taking George for a walk around the grounds, but he could have no legitimate reason for taking him through the gate into the car park. Luckily George was wearing a fairly presentable shirt and trousers, but his feet sported a giveaway pair of brown tweedy slippers. Well, now or never.

'Walk *quickly* to the red car,' he said to George, who complied without hesitation. 'Get in the back seat,' he ordered, and George did. Patrick got in beside him. Richard drove off, admirably repressing the urge to speed.

The four stood in the kitchen. 'Come here,' said Silas. George went over to him. Silas took both his hands and held them. Richard held his breath. Then he saw the change in George's face. The features were the same, but there was all the difference in the world. There was someone looking out through the eyes, someone alert, stubborn, truculent, normal. Normality spread through the kitchen, through the house.

George snatched his hands away from Silas's. 'I suppose I say thanks,' he said.

'No,' said Patrick, 'you don't need to do that.'

'Well, thanks anyway. For getting me back together. But it don't mean I like you. I don't. You're a pair of benders. And you're a blackie,' he said to Silas. 'Shouldn't wonder if you were a bender and all. I don't want any of your sort in my house.'

'But it isn't your house,' Patrick pointed out. 'Not any more.'

'I know that!' shouted George. 'D'you think I don't know that? Haven't I had to watch you, messing up my kitchen, ruining my nice pantry, making holes in the walls, God knows what all? I know it's not my house no more. They said I'd got to leave, and I couldn't leave. I couldn't stay, and I couldn't go. So I got stretched, and split, and I had to stop here and watch queers poncing about in my house where I was born. Don't know what my poor mum would have said.'

'Oh hell, where's Sylvia?' Richard muttered.

Sylvia's green van was stuck in traffic at Wanstead. June was getting agitated, pointing out that this wasn't the quickest way to Lamburne Street.

'George isn't there,' said Sylvia, shooting across on the amber on to the relatively uncongested Eastern Avenue.

'So where is he?' June demanded.

'I'm taking you to him,' said Sylvia evasively.

'Oh, you don't have to worry, I'm going,' George said. 'I'm grateful you got me back in one piece. It was orrible how things were, I never done it on purpose. But I wouldn't stay here with the likes of you even if you wanted me to. Poofs and blackies, I dunno, it's a different world.'

'It's a better world,' said Patrick gently, but George looked at him scornfully.

'I'm not going back to the orspital neither,' he said. 'I'll go down the Social, they'll have to fix me up with somewhere.'

'That may not be necessary,' said Richard. 'Your daughter …'

'*She* can't do nuffink,' said George. 'She's a good girl, my June, but that 'usband of hers –'

'That's just it,' said Richard, 'she's …'

The doorbell rang.

June stood in the kitchen doorway, gazing incredulously at her father.

'Dad?' she said hesitantly. 'Dad, is it you?' She ran to him and hugged him. 'Dad, it's really you, isn't it?'

George extricated himself from her embrace.

'Course it's me, oo did you think it was, you silly mare?'

Patrick laughed. 'They'll be all right,' he said.

'So will we,' said Richard.

CIRCLE OF SIX

Michael Ewers

Stone Gate Cottage is a normal kind of cottage by most people's standards. It is nothing special to look at, and there is nothing worthy of any great degree of remark within it either. Fittingly, there have never been any occupants that have given the place any 'character', nor any visitors distinguished enough to be worthy of mention.

I visit this particular cottage from time to time with a certain very select group of people, six of us in all. I suppose one might loosely call them friends, but they aren't people I usually mix with at other times. I first came here at the age of 27, when some might say I was in my prime; others might call me an over-eager whipper-snapper, and quite a few did indeed say just that. There were even one or two who went a great deal further.

There's really no point in my going into any great detail about myself, or any of the others, so I shall try to be brief. My main pastime would have been enjoying life, quote unquote, if you know what I mean. I would work at a job that required virtually no mental ability, just so that I had enough money in my pocket at the end of the week to enable me to join my friends for the obligatory Friday and Saturday night piss-ups, occasions that were more than they might seem to the untrained observer.

I, indeed we, my friends and I, used to know how to enjoy ourselves. Because of our various working-hours, our Friday night would start at about seven o'clock with a drink at each house we visited as we walked from the outskirts of town, picking up our friends one by one. Only one of them lived further out of the centre of town than I did, so the two of us would have had more to drink than the others by the time we got to the last guy's house. We'd hit the bars at around eight, and with a mixture of drinking, dancing, drinking, flirting, drinking, fighting and drinking we would be ready for the obligatory take-away by about midnight. This was the 'silly-hour'. It was as if somehow God had decided that any single guy out for a drink would lose control of his legs when the clock struck twelve. Anyway, we would have great fun on these nights, maybe topped off with a slanging match of some kind on the way home and, if it was a good night, we'd even have a mass vomiting session on someone's lawn – no one we knew of course.

Saturdays would have a slightly different formula, because Saturday nights were 'pulling' nights. On Saturdays my mates would meet up with the girls they'd chatted up on the Friday night – a bullet I would have to dodge carefully, since my idea of a date wouldn't exactly go down well with my mates. As people paired off, I'd become free to start chatting up someone more to my taste without the worry of being spotted. Whatever we got up to, we knew we would all soon be exchanging stories of what we'd done – of course as I told my story I'd have to change the gender of my 'partner'; a small price to pay for being able to have a social life. You'd be amazed at the things we'd get people to do under the influence of drink that they would never have agreed to when sober. Wow! I still can't help but smile at the things I got up to and the places too …

Suffice to say that I would have been referred to as a 'lad'. Not a bad thing to be called – I know of many people who've been called worse.

But now, to get back to the cottage: the other people who join me there are a sedate bunch, perhaps even a rather sober, and while I'm waiting for them to arrive I suppose I could tell you a little bit about them.

My name's Graham, by the way I suppose I should I should have mentioned that earlier. As I was saying, the others who visit the cottage with me are the quiet sort: three other guys and two women. The guys are Jim, Marshall and Daryn. The women are Renée and Jacqueline.

Jim is the teacher type. He did some teaching many years ago and now seems to think that everyone is his pupil – least that's certainly how it seems from the way he talks to people. Underneath he's a caring, heart-in-the-right-place kind of guy.

Marshall strikes me as the sort of guy whose brain was perhaps put in backwards. I don't mean that in a horrible way. It's just that he's a bit slow on the uptake sometimes.

Daryn's a mere teenager, prone to speaking before realising what it is he's saying. Over time he's become so self-conscious it's now increasingly difficult to get him to say anything at all.

Then there's Renée, who's a bit older than the rest of us. Kind of the mother figure of the group. She tends to raise her voice much of the time, even when she's just having a normal conversation – not that I've ever had a normal conversation with her. But then I suppose I've never had what you'd call a 'normal' conversation with any of them. Conversation never seems to happen at the cottage: it's almost an unwritten rule.

Finally, Jacqueline. She's only a year or so older than me, and we seem to get on quite well. My overriding impression of her is that she's very tall. Isn't it strange how you can see someone and think they're tall, and yet you see someone else of the same height and it doesn't even register?

Of course, there's probably lots more to tell, but I don't see the point. We don't talk much, and as our little get-together only lasts for half-an-hour or so, let's face it, you aren't going to get to know people that well in the occasional half-hour here, half-hour there. In addition to that, the experiences at the cottage have so profoundly challenged, and I suppose changed, all of us that none of us are really like ourselves any more Well, not when we're at the cottage, anyway.

I can't believe it was me once again who gets to pace around this damn place on my own waiting for the rest of them. Why am I always the one left wandering around?

Same dingy room.

We always use the same room.

I think this cottage in previous years had a very big family in it. It seems to have that feel. Like as if it's now relaxing, after having been bursting at the seams with the hustle and bustle of a big and very loud family. Funny how buildings give off vibes like that.

'You're here first again.'

That's the unmistakable voice of Renée.

'Yes, it seems to be the way of things,' I reply. I could of course comment on how everyone else is so tardy, but best not to ruffle feathers unnecessarily, especially so early in the evening.

'Well, Jim and Daryn are right behind me, so brace yourself.'

'Do we know what bee is in Jim's bonnet tonight?' I ask, not caring, for it is sure to be complete nonsense. I do feel sorry for Daryn; he's so young and he seems to feel obliged just to take the verbal explosion that Jim is likely to enter into if allowed. Maybe that's why Jim usually seeks Daryn out: he knows he won't tell him to shove a brick in his talking hole.

And there we have it. Jim's voice clearly audible. And I have just a matter of seconds left before he descends in all his glory.

'Get ready,' Renée says, a sly glint in her eye.

The conversation, well, more of a monologue really, becomes understandable seconds later. I look at Renée in sheer disbelief; I can't believe the degree of passion with which Jim is discussing the number of teats on the udders of cows.

As they enter, poor Daryn looks almost zombified by the conversation. His face lights up with the prospect of other company while Jim goes quiet, perhaps from the fear of being told he is talking about something which is often referred to as of the cow – or bull, perhaps?

'Well, I see we are gathering already,' Jim says in that jovial head-teacher type of way, the sort of thing where they wring their hands a little, and smile as if they are troubled with constipation, but don't want anyone to know.'

Now, how about we take our seats, so that when the last two get here we can get started as soon as possible. I have a good feeling about tonight. Energised. That's the word. I feel energised at the thought of tonight. I'm sure it's going to be a good one.'

Renée has her head down. She is already seated at the table, trying to clear her mind. She is into meditation in a big way, and I suppose she needs to be. Daryn and I exchange a glance as Jim noisily drags a chair over to the table, sitting himself down next to Renée. I feel sorry for her, but it is a half-hearted sort of sorrow, because at the same time I am so thankful that Jim hasn't decided to try to sit next to me. We are none of us great conversationalists. Our situation dictates that, but we do sometimes make the effort. It is Jim's conversation we dread. We are all aware of how much effort he puts into it, yet at the same time he is almost always talking the stuff of cesspools.

Marshall's arrival moments later is an understated affair. He enters, there are a few glances and that is that. He knows he has to be here, and he knows where 'here' is. That is enough for Marshall.

With his arrival, and his immediate move to seat himself to the other side of Renée, I think it best to take up my seat, and gesture Daryn to do the same. We are just one short, but, by the time we are seated, Jacqueline too is entering. No words are spoken; she sees us, pulls a seat to the table and completes the gathering.

I suppose to the outside observer we would appear an odd bunch but here we sit – yet again: six chairs around a dusty old table, waiting for Renée to signal that we are ready to start our little ritual. A ritual that we now go through six times every year.

Renée being the oldest, and perhaps the clearest of mind, is the one who assumes control now. She takes a deep breath, her chest fills noticeably, and she opens her eyes wider than I think is healthy. 'I think we can begin,' she announces.

All of us take our cue and start to hold hands in a circle around the table.

It is frowned on for anyone to speak from here on unless spoken to, so the room fills with a silence which we've all experienced so many times before. It is a unique silence, one of exhilaration, expectation and excitement, yet tainted with profound sadness and, for most of us, worry.

After a few minutes of silent concentration and channelling, Renée breaks the circle. 'It's no good. I can't get through to anything at all,' she complains.

'We still have time left,' Jim announces. He looks towards the rest of the group. 'We must concentrate harder, picture those we wish to contact.' He looks back to Renée. 'You will try again, won't you?'

After a glance at the rest of us, Renée concurs with a weary nod. She takes Jim's and Marshall's outstretched hands,-completing the circle once again.

There are moments during the next five to ten minutes when one or two of us are so close to contact that we can taste it, but, for reasons best known to powers greater than us, the whole thing ends without a successful contact being made. The circle breaks up, and the night's efforts are at an end.

'I just don't understand it,' Jim complains to himself. 'I was so looking forward to speaking to someone tonight.' His thoughts, expressed aloud, continue as he wanders out of the room and away.

To no one's surprise, Marshall says nothing. He just acknowledges us one by one with a glance, maybe a slight nod, and then he too goes on his way.

73

Jacqueline seems quite unfazed by our lack of success, so she also departs without a word, in fact without so much as a glance in my direction. I don't know whether anyone else gets better treatment.

Disappointment tends to quiet people down. Strangely, it is at times of such disappointments that people could best benefit from conversation. It's one of those things. That's human nature for you!

Daryn seems a little upset by the whole experience. Being so young, I think he misses the familial connection more keenly than the rest of us. Renée smiles at me as I step over to Daryn; she leaves me to try to say a few words. Not something in which I am well practised.

'It is very disappointing.'

He has remained seated, but looks up, maybe a little surprised at being spoken to. His eyes are filling up.

'You know this does happen. Sometimes it can be several visits between contact,' I explain.

'But my family were never believers in this,' he says softly.

'They don't have to believe, Daryn. If we can break through the barriers, then we make them believers.'

'I just hate knowing what's going on there. I think it'd be easier if I didn't,' he explains. 'And knowing that the most important person to me needs me more than ever.'

'It isn't easy, but we do get through to them sometimes.' With no reaction from him, it seems I'm not making my point. 'And when we do, then everything becomes so much clearer.'

'My friends and I used to do stuff like this … we used to try to contact the dead. It was fun then. Nothing ever happened, though.'

'That was fun; this is serious. It does work and it works both ways.' He is calming down. 'I promise you, we will do it. Who knows, you might even get to walk through your family's house. Jim did that once.'

His eyes light up. 'Really? He passed over completely?'

74

'You bet he did. I was right here and watched him move between here and there. He spoke directly to his son.'

'I wish I could do something like that. I wish I could tell everyone that I am all right. There's someone who really needs to hear that.'

'We all have people we need to speak to.'

'He blames himself for what happened. Fact is' – the eyes are starting to well up again – 'I'd have done anything for him. He needs to know I don't blame him.'

I put my arm on his shoulder. 'No one ever said being dead was easy, but we manage. As you will.'

After a few minutes we leave the old cottage together and talk for a while, an experience that isn't completely weird but is strange … I mean, there's not much call for conversation here.

COMPULSORY ASSISTANCE

Anne Stanesby

My story begins in May, May 2003. I was out there doing my bit for the local community, my feet and legs encased in a pair of giant waders in the middle of a slightly pongy pond. The surface of the pond was completely covered with a layer of duckweed which we were slowly entrapping between two floating booms and then removing with the assistance of a collection of plastic kitchen colanders.

It was peaceful except when passers-by stopped to cross-examine us.

'What yer doing?'

'Removing the duckweed.'

'Oh.'

'Come and help.'

That always got rid of them.

But one person just watched us silently. I didn't notice him at first. He was standing amongst the elder trees, and at first I mistook his face for just another white cauliflower-like sprig of elderflower. But then my eyes caught his, and I saw it was a person there. I couldn't see his body or his clothes, just his face. His hair was white, straight and slicked back. His face was puffy and pasty-coloured, almost featureless with a snub nose and regular chin. I could not tell the colour of his eyes but they seemed almost to glow as if they were boring right into me. Basically, he gave me the creeps.

Suddenly there was a whoop of excitement. Someone had found a tadpole, an excuse to stop for a chat.

'Did you see that man looking at us?'

'What man?'

'Over there.'

But he had gone.

The next person to make an exciting find was me. There were all sorts of things in that pond, and I proudly hauled aloft a wooden chairleg.

'Who shall I murder?'

'Not us!' they cried.

In the corner of my eye I thought I spotted that face again. I whirled around brandishing my chair leg in his direction. But he was not there after all.

They laughed at me, and we returned to work with our colanders.

When the time came to leave, we scrambled up the bank and hauled off the waders. I looked for my trainers and cursed because one was missing, I'd seen a fox earlier: I knew they like shoes. Why hadn't I hung them on a tree? I peered into the undergrowth. There it was – my lost shoe. Eagerly I stepped forward in my sock-clad feet. Disastrous. I trod straight on something sharp, something that went right into my foot. Well, it would do; that's what nails are for.

It could have been worse, but that grounded me at home for a while. I didn't miss much. No one else turned up next week either. They all went down with a bug. One way and another, we gave the pool a miss after that.

I enjoyed that sort of volunteering: it made a great change after being under constant observation in the hospital. It's amazing how, amongst the filth and litter, and general vileness of the city, it is possible to create a haven, an oasis of wild plants and wild creatures away from it all. I relished it, so I was not a happy bunny when, on turning up one week, I found our cherished site invaded by police personnel, police vehicles with flashing lights, and a collection of macho chaps with large cameras – the Press.

Amongst it all stood our co-ordinators. They looked uncharacteristically stressed.

'What happened?'

Speaking in whispers, they told me. The body of a teenage boy had been found floating in one of the ponds. The pond with the duckweed. Foul play was suspected.

'He couldn't have drowned; it's too shallow.'

'They want to know if we saw anything suspicious.'

'Anything?'

'Yes, anything.'

I thought of the man I alone had seen.

A few hours later I was sitting in the local police station completing an identikit picture. I didn't find it difficult at all; that face was firmly etched upon my memory, which was unusual for me. The CID man dealing with me was a calm, seen-it-all, heard-it-all type.

'Strange,' he said slowly. 'Very strange.'

'What is?'

'You said no one but you saw this particular gent, but we've had a number of other sightings of him reported to us, and over quite a period of time.'

'Oh, what I meant was that no one else with me saw him.'

'That's what's strange about it.'

'What do you mean?'

'That's what all the other chaps said. They weren't alone when they saw him, but none of their companions noticed him at all, which is why ...' he sighed.

'Why what?'

He looked straight at me.

'Which is why they didn't come to us before. It takes something like this.'

'I'm sorry but I didn't think. Well, what could I have said?'

'Not a lot, mate, or should I say not a lot that the plods on the desk would have taken note of.'

We parted on friendly terms. When we shook hands, I found out that he, like me, was a Mason.

A few days later our pond was drained. At least that got rid of the duckweed, but I still felt rather sad about it. Later we heard some human bones had been found.

The weeks went by, but of the teenager's murderer there was no sign. And no news of an arrest, either. It was rumoured that it might not even have been a murder at all. There were no marks of violence on the body, so it was said. He was probably high on something and just fell in.

That might have been that, had I not chosen to go for a stroll one day in Nunhead cemetery. A light breeze ruffled the branches of the trees. It had rained and rained, and the whole place was greener than I had ever seen it before. I went up to the ruined chapel, and sat there for a while. I felt sad. The blues were returning.

I had tried to drive them away, but they were coming back. I leapt up and strode down one of the grassy pathways, looking angrily at the graves. Masons were buried there; I recognised our symbol – the square and the compasses.

Suddenly the breeze picked up. Was a storm coming? There shouldn't be, the sun was shining. Why was I shivering?

One of the graves had a poem on it. I stopped to read it. The lettering was quite clear, whereas on many of the tombstones it was too worn to read easily:

Though your body be not whole,
Still united is your soul.
And though I may fall from grace,
I'll bring you to your resting place.

The tomb was that of a James Benson who had died before his sixteenth birthday, at the beginning of the twentieth century. Odd that the lettering was so clear. The grave was well tended too, which was strange when you thought how long ago James Benson had died. I was shivering even more now, while above me the trees shook, as if in the grip of a giant hurricane.

I looked up, and that was when I saw him again. It was him; I was sure of it. I could never forget that face; the man I had seen by the duckweed pond. He was staring at me urgently. It was as if he wanted something of me. He mouthed some words. 'Help me,' I thought it was, but when I blinked he had gone.

No human being could have vanished as fast as that. Was I seeing things? What was going on?

I went back to the entrance. It was Sunday and someone was at the portacabin. I wondered if he knew about James Benson.

'Well I do, in fact. It's rather a sad tale. Came to a sticky end in the Rosemary Dock area, I'm afraid. Entangled in a ship's rudder. They only found bits of him. I expect the rest of him is still somewhere around there. Someone's looking after the grave. Do you know who?'

'I don't, I'm afraid. 'Can't be the father, he was executed: he killed the man who owned the ship. Blamed him for his son's death … Sad, isn't it? Can't say that any members of the family have ever been in touch with us.'

I went home and thought about it all. Had I seen a ghost, the ghost of James Benson's father, still looking for his dead son's missing body bits? I thought about those bones, the ones the police had found in the pond. Were those James Benson's bones? What was left of Rosemary Dock was just round the corner. It was a possibility.

Did the ghostly father know that's where they were? Was he mounting guard on them? Deterring those who might do damage to them? I thought of my accident, my colleagues' illness and the death of the boy. Did James Benson's father want me to help him? He must have been a Mason like me. Maybe only Masons could see him. Masons are supposed to help each other. Maybe he would have expected me to be of assistance. But what exactly was I supposed to do? The CID man was a Mason too. Could I

80

confide in him? What if I told him of my suspicions, and that I thought the bones in the pond were those of James Benson? But then what could he do about it? Arrange for a DNA test to prove it? Or would he privately conclude that I was a nutter? Worse still, would he get on to my psychiatrist, the one who had stuffed me full of pills? The one who nearly made me have ECT. Yes, of course he would.

There's a limit to Masonic loyalty. I of all people could not assist.

They came for me a few weeks later. They said I'd killed that boy in the duckweed pond. They say they can prove it through DNA testing. They know I'm gay, and they know about my psychiatric history.

'You queers are all the same,' said the friendly CID man. 'Nutty as a fruit cake.'

I had made a mistake. I had not realised that James's father was demanding compulsory assistance.

FRIEND OF THE SPIRIT

Michael Harth

It was only the fact that he fancied Scott rotten that had persuaded Luke to make the promise in the first place. Now, as he sat opposite him in Scott's little flat, the attraction was, if anything, stronger, even though he had uncomfortable forebodings about what the fulfilment of that promise might entail. He knew Scott had an extensive background of psychedelic experiences behind him, but he was still very dubious about the effect this particular stuff would produce. Even more worrying was the thought of the part that he knew he would be called on to play.

In spite of regular offers from Scott to join him when he was trying out other mind-altering drugs, and the thought that if he did so it would almost certainly lead to greater intimacy, he had so far steered completely clear, his experience of recreational substances being confined to the occasional joint. This time, though, it would be necessary for him to be involved if the drug was to be used in accordance with the native tradition, and he knew with sick certainty that if – or almost certainly when – Scott tried to persuade him to do his bit, he would be unable to say no.

It wasn't as if Scott were any Adonis. Shorter than average, with rather coarse, peasant-style features, he was not the type to cause heads to turn for a second look, but Luke found something irresistibly fascinating in his muscular frame, while his eyes kept returning to the tight jeans Scott wore, which certainly did nothing to hide what appeared to be an impressive masculinity.

It was indeed difficult to fit his physical appearance with his obsessive interest in other-worldly experiences. He had at one time belonged to a Lodge, where he had investigated a number of occult techniques: Luke had been in town when he was trying out sex magic, and Scott had been keen for his assistance in this, but with his usual caution he had hastily declined.

Presumably none of these avenues had given him what he wanted, for after that he had then turned to experiments with mind-altering substances, quickly running the gamut of all those available. First it had been naturally occurring hallucinogens: several species of magic mushroom, native and imported, morning glory, and a whole host of other plants whose names Luke couldn't remember. Many of them Scott had grown himself, so that at one time his conservatory looked more like a greenhouse.

After them he moved on to synthetics, from LSD to the phenylamines and then the tryptamine family. It seemed that none of them had provided him with the experience he was looking for, and it was at that time that he had pressed Luke, who as a social anthropologist regularly went on field trips to South America, to look out for others.

He was pretty certain that, if he bargained with Scott, the plant in return for a night of passion, Scott would agree immediately with no fuss. But he couldn't bring himself to be so blatant, and Scott, though always friendly and apparently pleased to see him, had never shown any sign of reciprocating his feelings. None the less, Scott had regularly been the central figure in night-time fantasies while he was on his recent trip, and seeing him in the flesh no way lessened the spell he cast.

Once he was settled, Scott made him a cup of coffee, but he was so obviously impatient to see what Luke had brought back from his travels that, with a slight sigh, Luke opened his case and took out the carefully labelled packets. First were samples of *anadenanthera peregrina*, used on its own by several tribes of Amazonian Indians as a snuff, but he had also included *banisteriopsis caapsi*, since the two together were the basis of the widely used drink called *ahayuasca*.

He looked hopefully at Scott, but Scott was not interested. Not only had he tried this particular combination, but the visions it produced, though rewarding in themselves, had been preceded by bouts of severe vomiting which had left him physically exhausted, and he was not in a hurry for a repeat of the experience if there was some less unpleasant way of gaining a similar sort of result.

Several species of *datura* and *brugmansia* were similarly passed over, since the dose required to produce hallucinogenic effects was dangerously near the toxic level. When similar effects could be obtained much more safely, Scott could see no point in trying them. Luke's last hope was *yopo*, a red resin taken from under the bark of a tree. But though Scott had never used it, he knew that the active constituent was similar to that in one of the plants he had grown himself, so he wasn't interested, especially as Luke, when he contacted Scott on his return, had unwisely hinted that he had something of exceptional interest.

Cursing himself mentally for being a blabbermouth, Luke was now reduced, reluctantly, to showing his last exhibit. Many, if not most, of the native tribes occupying the area he had recently travelled through used various of the mind-bending substances nature provided, and so far as he knew fatal results were unknown among them. But this particular plant was regarded as dangerous even by those who made use of it. A vine, it had not so far been botanically classified, and its use was restricted to a small area along the Amazon basin, among a tribe who called themselves the Retsiwana, little studied so far by anthropologists.

The only reason Luke had ventured to their otherwise unrewarding region was because he had heard about the plant, which was regarded unfavourably by adjoining tribes, all of whom used some form of mind-bending brew, but still shunned this one. The Retsiwana, in return, despised their neighbours for using what they disparagingly called baby-brews, though even they treated the plant with respect, so that its use was always a ceremonial matter at which all the males of the tribe were present.

Their particular tribal deity was contacted – probably invoked would be a more accurate term, he thought – by means of the drug. This was an extremely risky business in which the unsuccessful, who were said to have been rejected by the god, lost their reason.

'There's usually someone willing to take the chance,' Luke explained. 'Whether because he genuinely wishes to contact the spirit world, or because he fancies the authority it will give him over the rest of the tribe, or just because he doesn't fancy the life of an ordinary male, I don't know. If there isn't, it's up to the chief to select one of the lads of suitable age, but this is rarely necessary, even though only about one in ten of the candidates are successful. The rest lose their marbles, and end up in a special house where the women care for them.'

Scott examined the piece of stalk, and the dried leaves attached to it, with cautious interest. Some of his previous experiences had been less than pleasant, but they hadn't dented his enthusiasm for further investigation.

'Did you observe anybody trying it?' he enquired.

Luke nodded.

'And what was the result?'

'I was only allowed to watch from some distance, but a blind man would have known what was happening,' Luke explained. 'It looked to me as if the candidate drank the whole of the brew, but his companion – each candidate has another lad with him, who is known as the "friend of the spirit" – finished off whatever was left. Then, after about twenty minutes, the candidate started shivering and trembling, and soon after he began babbling so fast that I couldn't get the gist of what he was saying, as my knowledge of the language is extremely limited. I suspect, though, that a lot of it was nonsense, not real words at all: he was obviously terrified, and seeing some pretty unpleasant visions.

'They let him go on like this for some half-an-hour, while the other one just stared into space, occasionally interjecting a few unintelligible words. When it became obvious that the main one hadn't made it, the chief nodded to two of his henchmen, and they carted him off to the hut on the edge of the compound reserved for those who didn't get through. There were only a couple of others in there; none of those who fail last long, on average a couple of years, and judging by what I saw of them it's a merciful release.'

'What about the friend?' Scott asked.

'He was taken to a hut, and as far as I know was all right after a couple of days,' Luke told him.

'You're not exactly encouraging,' Scott complained with a mixture of amusement and annoyance.

'No', Luke agreed. 'The natives call it devil-weed, and I think that's a pretty fair name for it. My advice to you is to leave it well alone. Or else send it to a lab, have it analysed so that you know what the active principle is, and then decide if you want to take it any further. At least then you'd have control over the dosage, and could start off at a low level, instead of plunging straight in at the deep end.'

Scott knew very well that this was good advice, but there was a reckless streak in his nature which meant that he liked to take risks, and though sometimes the results had been scary, he had always come out the other end more or less unscathed. So both of them knew that sooner or later, almost certainly sooner, he would be imitating the Retsiwana Indians, and finding out if he too could communicate with the spirit world.

In fact Luke had a double motive for not wanting Scott to try out the drug. Besides the concern for his welfare, there was another more personal reason which he had so far omitted to mention. This was because he knew that Scott would ask him to act as his 'friend', and he had no wish to share in the experience even slightly.

It was a point of honour among the Retsiwana that the candidate would drain the draught, leaving only the lees for his companion, but even that small amount had proven sufficient to affect them, and so Luke was uncomfortable, not to say worried, by the thought of what might happen to him if Scott wished to make the experiment. He hadn't thought at the time to find out just why the second man was considered necessary, an oversight he now regretted, and this added to his disquiet.

He left Scott's flat shortly after, both uneasy and unhappy. He regretted now his promise to Scott to bring him back a sample of anything in the hallucinogenic line he came across in his travels. If it hadn't been that Scott had proved himself to be exceptionally stable and well-balanced, emerging in one piece from all the various experiments he had tried, he doubted whether he would ever have let him have the stuff. Even now he wasn't sure he had done the right thing: on the other hand a promise was a promise, and he wanted very much to have Scott feeling obliged to him.

Scott dithered for a few days before taking the plunge, but he knew very well he was only postponing the moment: there was no way he was going to miss this chance. None of the various other substances he had imbibed had provided him with the transcendental experience he was looking for. A number of the accounts he had read of others describing their reactions under the influence of this or that drug had fired his hopes, but when he investigated for himself, the results had invariably been something of a let-down.

But Scott was not the type to rush headlong into anything: like all the best explorers, he believed in preparing himself as fully as possible before he actually ventured. So he quizzed Luke thoroughly about the actual ceremony during which the postulants drank the potion, learning that they fasted for a couple of days beforehand, and then drank only water.

He was perfectly well aware that Luke had the hots for him, and so he knew he would have little trouble persuading him to act as his spiritual brother. When he asked, Luke did his very best to persuade Scott against what he described as 'this extremely foolhardy experiment', but when Scott flatly refused to change his mind, he reluctantly agreed to do what was necessary. He had already explained to Scott that even the successful ones rarely lived more than a few years after the ceremony: the tribe's explanation was that the constant communion with the god ate them away, which was why a constant supply of new postulants was required.

It hadn't struck Luke as sufficient recompense that, during their brief reign as Shaman, their lightest wish was literally law, and they were waited on with complete and utter devotion. Judging by what Luke had seen of them, they didn't exist in a state which allowed them to get much satisfaction from these attentions.

Although Luke was reasonably conversant with most of the languages used in the area he had been working in, the dialect used by the Retsiwana gave him a lot of trouble, and he had had particular difficulty with the shaman. It had only been with the greatest difficulty that Luke had persuaded him to let him have the few leaves he had brought back: in fact, if it weren't that the man had a weakness for whisky, he doubted that he'd have got them.

Then, once they had been handed over, he seemed to regret what he had done, and either didn't understand when Luke asked him how to prepare it, or didn't want to reveal his secrets; Luke couldn't tell. But the result was that he had no information about how much of the vine was used to make a dose.

So Scott would be venturing into uncharted territory. The few leaves he had brought back were quite likely only enough for one experiment, possibly two if he was lucky. Luke had been told that not only was the vine quite a rare plant, but no one outside the tribe had ever used it, and that if they did it would destroy their spirit, though Scott was too sure of himself to let that worry him.

Having no desire to go through the vomiting that had accompanied his experience with *ahayuasca*, Scott decided it was safer to follow the natives' recommendations, and fast for two days beforehand. Not being used to it, he was quite light-headed when he was ready to try out the drug. Luke had not thought it necessary to emulate him, but he had restricted himself to very light meals.

Since Luke was to be involved in the process, even if only peripherally, they brought in a third person to observe and if necessary help. This was a friend of Scott's called Francis, who had joined Scott on a number of previous occasions, so that he was fully aware of what would be going on, and what he might need to do.

A veteran of many similar occasions, Scott prepared the brew carefully, using only about half of the amount of plant he had been given, and ending up with a dark green liquid which, when he took a tentative sip, tasted fairly disgusting, but no more so than many others he had sampled. Finally it was time. He had donned a loose smock, though Luke's only concession was an open-necked shirt.

Scott had diluted the preparation with green tea, which he drank regularly, both because he thought it good for him and because he had grown to like it. The idea was to make the brew less unpalatable, and Luke, having been warned that it would taste foul, thought it a good idea to empty the rest of the pot into the small amount waiting for him in his glass. Then Scott took a tentative mouthful, swallowed it down, and waited for a few moments. Mercifully, he didn't feel sick, so he drank the rest in small amounts, and lay back to await the onset of its effects.

Luke did his best to keep up with him, using his own much weaker potion, and by the time he had finished what was in his glass, he had begun to feel quite light-headed. With an effort, he looked over at Scott, who was lying flat out, looking totally relaxed. Francis, meanwhile, kept a watchful eye on both of them. One of the main reasons Scott regularly chose him to be around was that he was a trained nurse, and always brought along a hypodermic syringe ready loaded with a dose of tranquilliser, for use as a last resort – he knew that Scott would be very cross if it was used other than in a serious emergency.

By the time an hour or so had elapsed without anything happening, he had begun to feel bored. He couldn't tell whether Scott was just relaxing, had dropped off to sleep, or had been rendered unconscious by the drug, while Luke was sitting there staring into space, and Francis didn't like to disturb him. But then, still with his eyes closed, Scott began to babble in some foreign tongue. Francis had a nodding acquaintance with half-a-dozen European languages, and he didn't think it sounded like any of them.

However, when Luke, also without moving or changing his expression, appeared to be answering him in what did sound to him like the same language, but in a different voice, higher and almost entirely toneless, prickles began to run up and down his spine. Too late, he thought they should have had a tape recorder to hand. When the conversation, if that was what it was, continued, he got up and hunted for one. He soon discovered a portable cassette recorder, but there was no tape in it, and by the time he found one, there was no more speech. Soon after the two men both fell asleep.

When Luke woke from the sleep the drug had induced, he had no clear remembrance of the experience, just some vaguely unpleasant recollections, and Francis judged it best not to tell him what he had witnessed. Scott was still out, but Luke didn't want to stay around till he awoke, so he told Francis he was feeling tired, and went home.

He wasn't sorry not to hear from Scott for the next couple of days, but then that evening he was asked to go round, though it was more like a summons. His obsession with Scott had been considerably diminished, but nonetheless he obediently went round. The Scott who opened the door to him seemed in some way different from the one he had seen just a few days ago. There was no social chit-chat, no offer of a drink: instead he was led straight into the bedroom, where he saw some lumps of what he presumed was charcoal burning in a brazier, while the room was full of a heady, spice-like odour. He was instructed as to what was required of him: only a few days ago, this would have seemed like the fulfilment of his deepest desire, but now he felt a strange reluctance.

Nevertheless, he listened carefully, after which he stripped off and lay on the bed, whereupon Scott mounted him and worked away tirelessly. After some considerable time, when Luke had been brought to a high pitch of physical stimulation, he was directed to focus, in the way that had been explained to him, all the energy that had been created. Scott was no doubt doing the same, for to Luke's exhausted awareness there seemed to form in the smoke what he quickly recognised as a likeness of the tribal deity of the Retsiwana.

Presumably Scott was seeing a similar hallucination, for he addressed it in the local dialect, not that this seemed odd to Luke at the time. But he had clearly been affected at some subconscious level, for he found himself answering, in a voice totally unlike his own. It was as if he had been taken over, while his real self was pushed to the back of his consciousness, for the conversation continued for some considerable time.

Eventually it seemed to be over; he felt the invader withdraw almost physically, and then he was once more in control of himself. Scott took a little longer to come out of whatever state he had been in, but when he did he was in a mood almost of exaltation. His eyes were shining, and he told Luke 'That was something like. He has promised to speak with me regularly, so you're going to be seeing a lot of me.'

He laughed boisterously.

'What do you mean?' Luke asked, with a sense of foreboding.

'As my spirit-friend, you are his mouthpiece. But then each time I speak with him, you get what you want, so we'll both be happy.'

But in fact, now that Luke had experienced Scott's lovemaking, he no longer felt the same about him. Luke was basically a romantic: love was more important to him than sex, and the sort of sex he liked was relaxed and comfortable: he didn't care for Scott's extremely physical style. Scott was an animal, he reflected uncomfortably as he made his way home; at the moment his main feeling towards him was one of revulsion, and he knew he didn't want to see him again in a hurry.

A few evenings later, he settled himself in his most comfortable chair, looking forward to a quiet evening at home with a book: he might even watch the television, he thought, should there be, by some remote chance, something worth his attention. But then he felt himself being summoned, and soon he was on his way to Scott's flat.

TAXI TO HEATHROW

Kathryn Bell

'Taxi! Take me to Heathrow, quickly!'

Clare put the phone down. The third time tonight, and twice last night. The first two times it happened, Clare had conscientiously explained that yes, she could send a cab to take the caller to Heathrow, but she needed an address. The caller – who sounded like an elderly woman – had become agitated, and repeated her request for a taxi to Heathrow before putting the phone down. A lunatic or a hoaxer. One of those things you have to put up with when you work for a minicab firm.

No. Why the hell should she put up with it? She dialled 1471.

'Femcabs here,' she said sweetly. 'Did anyone want a cab to Heathrow?'

'Oh, I'm *so* sorry,' said the voice on the other end. A rather pleasant-sounding female voice. 'It's my aunt Stella. She's getting on, you know, and – well – I try to keep her away from the phone, but I can't have my eye on her every minute, and she's quite clever at taking advantage when my back's turned. Would you be kind enough to humour her? Just tell her you're sending a cab in ten minutes? It won't go on for much longer, she'll stop it in a few days. It's something that gets into her about this time of year.'

Well, at least it wasn't malicious, just simple lunacy. Clare agreed to do as she was asked, and left a note for the other operators.

Two days later, Clare was out on the road when she got a call to take a passenger from Plaistow to Chingford.

'I hope you can get there by half five,' said the passenger, a nice-looking woman of about thirty. 'The garage shuts then, and I really do want to pick up my car today. I wouldn't have had a hope of getting there in time by bus.'

'Do my best,' said Clare, wondering where she had heard that Liverpool accent before. A character on Brookside perhaps?

'Of course it's daft going to a garage so far away,' the passenger went on, 'but I used to live in Chingford, only moved to Plaistow six months ago, and Monty's Motors know me and my car. I get a fair deal from them. I hate going to a garage I don't know, I'm sure they take advantage, don't you think?'

'Too true,' muttered Clare bitterly, then, suddenly remembering where she had heard that voice before, she said 'You're Stella's niece, aren't you?'

'That's right,' said the passenger. 'It was you I talked to the other night? Thanks for putting up with auntie, she's why I called your firm. I thought as you got the aggro, you might as well get the fare. My name's Nerina, by the way. Oh look, here we are, ten minutes to spare. Thanks so much, you're a sweetie.'

Clare had had some talkative passengers before, but none quite like Nerina. And not many as good-looking. Rather a pity she's got a car, Clare thought; probably I won't see her again.

When she did see her, it was in the last place she would have expected. Anthea had asked Clare to swap shifts with her, leaving Clare with an unaccustomed Tuesday evening off. Tuesday was Women's Night at the local gay pub, the Lord Kitchener, and Clare settled herself at a table with her half-pint of cider plus a cheese and pickle sandwich. Usually the place was full of men, but tonight ... Clare was thinking she should arrange to have Tuesday free more often, when half-a-dozen women came in and crowded around the bar. One blonde head looked familiar.

Nerina, having obtained her drink, turned from the bar and spotted Clare.

'Hi, mind if I sit here? Nice to see you again. How are

94

you?'

'Fine,' said Clare. 'And you? How's Aunt Stella?'

'Oh, she's okay, calmed down now, not making any more daft phone calls. Poor Stella, I shouldn't say that, she's had a hard time. It's a tragic story. Lost her girl friend in an accident, years ago, never really got over it. Can I get you another drink? Sure? Okay. Well, she had this gorgeous Aussie girlfriend. They lived together for years not far from here, in East Ham. They bought each other those rings with lesbian symbols on, you know, they were so popular back in the seventies. One Christmas her girlfriend had to go home, death in the family or something. She was due back early in January and Stella went to the airport to meet her, but the plane crashed and there were no survivors. Oh look, I need another spritzer, sure I can't get you something? Right, cider and a bag of salt and vinegar, coming up.'

Nerina came back with the drinks and resumed her tale. 'Imagine it, you've been separated from your lover for weeks, you go to the airport to bring her home, all happy and excited to be seeing her again, but when you get there, there's all this commotion and rumours about a crash. You think, dozens of planes coming and going all the time, it can't be the one you're meeting, but all the same you start to be worried.

'Then you find it *was* that plane, but you still hope she might have survived, then you learn there aren't any survivors, but you still think there could be a mistake – well, you can imagine. When it finally sunk in, Stella was devastated. For months she wouldn't go out, wouldn't go to work, would barely eat, some days she wouldn't even bother to wash or dress herself.

'Then after about six months she started to pull herself together, went back to work, got on with her life. She was never her old self again, but she was coping. It was only after she retired that she went a bit strange. Every year, after Christmas, around the time the decorations are coming down, she thinks she's got to go to Heathrow to meet the plane. It only lasts a few days, and the rest of the time she's quite okay. When I came down to Chingford, I brought her to live with me; we've got no other family left.'

'That was very generous of you,' Clare remarked.

'No, it's worked out fine, I'm the one who benefits. Stella does most of the housework, she's in when the meter readers and the delivery men come, and when I get home from work I sit down to my supper without having to cook. Life without a care, it's like being a man.'

Clare laughed. 'We should all have an Aunt Stella,' she said.

'True enough. I only have to look after her for those few days in a year. The rest of the time she looks after me. Another drink?'

About a week later, Clare was on telephone duty in the office when a woman came to the door. About forty-five, Clare thought, short blonde hair just going grey, face that had once been pretty and was still quite presentable.

'Can you help me please? I need a cab to Heathrow, urgently.'

'Sorry love, the drivers are all busy and I can't guarantee anything for half an hour at least.'

The woman twisted her hands nervously. 'It's really important,' she said. 'I have to meet someone and ... *please* try.'

'All right, tell you what I'll do. I'm off duty in ten minutes. When my relief turns up I'll take you myself. I could do with a bit of a run, been stuck in the office all day.'

Now I know why the drivers are all busy, Clare thought. They're all out on the Westway, along with half the cars in London. The passenger was having kittens in the back seat, fretting about being late, for heaven's sake. Anyone would think she was trying to *catch* a plane instead of just meeting one. The person she was meeting wouldn't be going anywhere. Clare kept her mouth shut; no point in getting into an argument with a passenger. They would get there when they got there.

It was raining when they arrived at Heathrow. Crowds of people were milling about under black umbrellas.

'Judy! Judy! Over here!' shouted the passenger, literally jumping up and down.

A tall, sun-tanned woman whose only luggage was a backpack ran up and embraced the short blonde.

'Have you been waiting long?' asked the blonde.

'Years,' said Judy. 'Well, it *felt* like years.'

They both laughed and hugged each other, for what Clare thought an embarrassingly long time.

The traffic seemed bent on making amends for the difficult journey to Heathrow. The trip back to East Ham went like a dream; the lights all turned green at Clare's approach, there was hardly any traffic, and certainly no jams. The two in the back seat talked quietly but incessantly; they must have had a hell of a lot of news to catch up on.

'Well, here we are: Mitcham Road,' said Clare. 'What number did you say again?'

Silence.

Clare turned round in her seat. The two women had disappeared, backpack and all, as if they had never been there.

Clare had intended to go straight home after dropping her passengers, but now she felt so fired up she had to go and let out her anger to somebody. How could she have let that happen, after all her years' experience? She'd thought the women so nice, and they looked so happy. Yes, they might well look happy, planning a free ride back from Heathrow. No wonder the pig came to the office instead of telephoning; Clare should have known she was up to no good. She drove to the Femcabs office and unburdened herself to Anthea.

'And what I can't understand,' she ranted, 'is that I never stopped once on the way back. The lights were in my favour all the way, I didn't have to stop at a crossing, so how did they just disappear?'

'You must have slowed down to turn a corner or something,' suggested Anthea, 'and they hopped out then.'

'Yes, well, I just hope they left plenty skin on the tarmac, the thieving ratbags.'

'Oh, come on, Clare, I know you're upset, but it's happened to all of us.'

'Not after sixteen years of cabbing, it hasn't. Not all the way to Heathrow and back, has it? *Has it?*'

'Well, no,' Anthea admitted, 'not as far as that. Oh look, I nearly forgot, this came for you. Someone dropped it in while you were gone.'

The envelope, addressed simply to 'Clare,' contained a card with 'Thank You' in silver lettering above a picture of a bunch of violets on the front. Inside, it said 'Thank You' again, in blue letters this time, and underneath, handwritten in violet ink, 'for being so understanding about auntie. I thought I should let you know, it won't happen any more, because Stella passed away this morning. It was a heart attack, quite sudden. I'll miss her, but I won't be sad for her. Her life hadn't been much fun since Judy died. See you at the Kitchener sometime? Nerina.'

Well, that put Clare's troubles into perspective. Poor Stella, she thought. And poor Judy, too. Judy, wasn't that the name of one of those freeloading bitches? It brought Clare's grievance back to her mind, and by the time she got home she was seething again. All the way to Heathrow and back – for *nothing* …

But in the morning, cleaning inside her car ready for the next shift, she found two gold rings, each bearing the emblem of linked female symbols, lying on the back seat.

ICENI 27

Miles Martlett

To those who knew him, it seemed both sad and ridiculous that Brett should have decided his life was over when he was not much past thirty, but to Brett it seemed so obvious as to be inevitable. He wasn't even bitter about it, but then what had he to be bitter about? For nearly ten years he had had the love of a man he adored, and when Gordon was taken from him in that car accident, he accepted that he would never again experience that sort of happiness.

Those of Gordon's friends who had known the two of them together found it especially ludicrous, for they knew that this was all founded on a lie. So far from it being a romantic union of two souls in perfect harmony, Gordon had admitted to them that he wasn't in love with Brett. He had initially picked him up because, in addition to his being a good-looking young man, there was something appealing about him.

It had not been a particularly interesting encounter for Gordon, since Brett was quite unable to satisfy him, and on top of that was too sexually inexperienced to realise that Gordon hadn't found it worthwhile. But Gordon, one of whose weaknesses was a tendency to let people down lightly, had made him a coffee afterwards, and listened to his life-story, which in essence was not very dissimilar from those of thousands of young men brought up in a conventional household, and slow to realise their true nature.

There was something quite appealing in the lad's naïvety, while he himself was so impressed with Gordon's greater sophistication that the time flew by, and before he realised it, it was too late for Brett to take the tube home. Gordon knew he should have sent him home in a taxi, but the lad so obviously didn't want to leave that he hadn't the heart, and Brett ended up staying the night.

That meant he got screwed again: it was marginally more interesting than the first time, but this was because he gave himself so completely to Gordon. Unfortunately he still had no idea how to make it a satisfying experience, and Gordon couldn't bring himself to instruct him, thinking that would be the last time.

Not a romantic himself, he was unable to appreciate Brett's feelings about their meeting, and so he was more than a little surprised, when he answered his doorbell a couple of evenings later, to find Brett on the doorstep. Gordon had been debating with himself whether or no to go out and get a bit of trade, but Brett's appearance decided him not to bother, and he invited him in.

Brett explained that he had forgotten to ask for Gordon's phone number, but he had enjoyed Gordon's company so much that he had just come along on the offchance, and he hoped Gordon didn't mind. Gordon was far too soft-hearted to tell him otherwise, and as the lad chatted, he kept thinking that he should get rid of him and go out, hopefully to find someone who understood sex.

At the same time he recalled how regularly his pick-ups had proved inadequate in the sack, ending with his returning home disappointed and wishing he hadn't bothered. The net result was that the time slipped away and Brett again stayed the night. This time Gordon decided he'd better show him a few things, so he gave him one of his fairly expert blow-jobs. Brett was out of his mind with pleasure and delight, but unfortunately, when he repaid the compliment, it was immediately obvious he hadn't paid any attention to Gordon's actual technique, and so Gordon knew that he was no kind of sensualist.

It was probably partly guilt over his relentless pursuit of sex that contributed to Gordon's failure to discourage Brett, and there was also a certain satisfaction in the fact that Brett so obviously adored him. Then he was a strikingly good-looking guy, regularly attracting attention when he went out, and Gordon could not but enjoy the reflected glory, feeling that it must considerably improve his stock to have pulled such a stunner.

Brett was round at his place so often that eventually Gordon accepted the inevitable and suggested that he should move in. Brett was quite domesticated, so now Gordon had the luxury of having his meals prepared for him, his clothes ironed – he was too impatient ever to bother with such things – while various little jobs around the house, that he regularly put off because he hated doing them, were now attended to.

Gordon had always had a lot of interests, and was active in a number of them, serving on committees and regularly making himself available when help was needed, so that Brett soon got used to him frequently going out, while he was quite content to stay home and watch the television. That was something he loved, but it was quite difficult when Gordon was around, since he had very little time for it, and in particular hated having it on except when there was a programme he particularly wanted to watch – an infrequent occurrence.

His various activities, however, made it comparatively easy for Gordon to do a spot of cruising after his official business was concluded, and in this way he contrived not to be too bothered by the unexciting sex he had with Brett, though not with any great frequency. Sometimes he would feel he was trapped, and had settled for second-best, but the mood wouldn't last long when he recalled that none of his previous affairs had been any more satisfactory, while Brett was such a sweet lad, and so useful, that he couldn't bring himself to hurt his feelings.

It was getting on for ten years later when the police brought Brett the news of Gordon's death. He hardly reacted at first: it was as if he had been frozen, and for some days he went around like a zombie. Even the thought that he would have more than sufficient money to allow him to live decently – about four years earlier, Gordon, in one of his fits of making plans, had got them both to take out life insurance, each naming the other as the beneficiary – was no consolation. Brett had grown so accustomed to being around Gordon, who had gradually become as much father as boyfriend, that he couldn't take in his loss.

A couple of days after the news had arrived, Gordon's best friend Carson came round to see him. Wisely, he didn't attempt to cheer Brett up, reasoning that he would have to work through his sorrow in his own way and his own time. But he told him he wouldn't need to move out of the house, for Gordon had willed it to Brett only a year or so before, and which he had left with Carson for safe-keeping.

Gordon's sister was clearly none too pleased at this, as was plain enough when she came to town for the funeral, but her two children, who had both achieved successful careers, and also were less uptight about their uncle's proclivities, expressed themselves as perfectly happy with the arrangement, and grateful for the couple of thousand each that Gordon had left them. As the weeks turned into months, Brett's picture of Gordon imperceptibly changed, all his less attractive qualities vanishing into limbo, till all that was remembered was his kindness, his generosity, and his appetite for life.

Their builds were too different for him to be able to wear any of Gordon's clothes, but he wouldn't throw any of them out; it would have felt like throwing a part of Gordon away. The house also remained just as it had been when Gordon was alive: if he had to repair or repaint any part, he made sure to do it in exactly the same style.

Though his family had moved to Dublin when he was a young boy, Brett was still at heart a country lad. After having lived in London for twelve years or so, he had acquired a thin veneer of sophistication, so that he had been able to make the effort to keep up with Gordon's friends, even though he didn't feel he had anything in common with them. They were all nice to him, but he sometimes felt as if they were humouring him: all except Carson, who genuinely seemed to like him. He was the only one with whom Brett felt he could be himself.

By the time several months had passed, Brett had settled into his new life, life without Gordon. He rarely went out, and even when he was persuaded by one of Gordon's old friends to go out for a drink, a couple of hours was more than enough, and he would be impatient to get home. He had long ago lost contact with all the folk he knew before Gordon came on the scene, but as they had been only casual acquaintances, and he had known they and Gordon would have nothing in common, that hadn't bothered him.

Carson came round to see him regularly, and Brett was always pleased when he called. He kept urging Brett to make a new life for himself, and not dwell in the past, but Brett would just smile and say he was perfectly happy. So Carson, who didn't like nagging people, would leave it till his next visit, when he would get the same answer. After a while, Brett did get to thinking Carson had a point, but he felt that to do as Carson suggested would be betraying his memories of Gordon, so he never did anything about it.

Gordon had spent a lot of time on his computer, writing and playing games mostly, so far as Brett was aware. He himself had never had one, but Gordon set him up his own screen and showed him how to use it. Apart from writing letters, when he always used it because both his spelling and his handwriting were pretty appalling, he rarely bothered. Gordon loved games of all sorts, and had tried to get Brett interested, but without much success, though occasionally he would have a go at the Mah-jong programme Gordon had loaded for him.

There was very little on his desktop, whereas Gordon's had been covered in icons, but he had never had a chance to look at it in detail, for it was protected by a password which he didn't know.

Brett did sometimes wonder what Gordon had on his screen that had to be hidden from everyone else, but when he mentioned his doubts one time, Gordon explained smoothly that it was to make sure no one accidentally deleted or corrupted any of his files. Brett accepted the explanation, even though he rather imagined that Gordon had one or two things up there that he wouldn't have wanted Brett to see, chief among them being porn.

Brett wasn't exactly a prude, but he wasn't very interested in that kind of thing. He knew that Gordon was a lot more sexual than he was, and he also knew that, before settling down with Brett, he had been around a good deal, but though he had suspected Gordon was dabbling elsewhere, he had preferred not to know about it.

It was several months after Gordon's death that, one evening, Brett was in the bathroom enjoying a leisurely bath. Some of the steam from the bath had condensed on the mirror, as it regularly did, and Brett idly gazed at it when he got out and began towelling himself. Then figures began to appear on the mirror surface, as if a finger were tracing them, and as Brett watched, half-hypnotised, there appeared, one by one, the letters ICENI, followed by the numerals 27.

Like all good Irish boys, Brett was superstitious, and so he had little difficulty in accepting this as some sort of message. They immediately reminded him of the Old Testament story, and certainly he had no more idea what they meant than King Belshazzar had had in his day. Unlike that king, however, there was no one Brett could think of consulting to explain what it meant: it conveyed absolutely nothing to him, and though he racked his brains all that evening, he was no wiser by the time he went to bed. He wasn't the type to continue puzzling over something so apparently meaningless, and by the next morning he had more or less dismissed it.

But a week or so later, he was combing his hair in the hall mirror when the hairs at the back of his neck bristled, and then the same combination of letters and numbers appeared on the wall behind him. He started disbelievingly for a few moments, then turned round to look at the actual wall, but was nothing unusual was to be seen there, and when he looked in the mirror again, they were no longer there.

This second time made it seem much more urgent that he should find out what they meant. He went through everything he could think of, and then turned to Gordon's papers. It was when he was examining the entries in Gordon's diary for the second time that he struck gold. Gordon had not, so far as he knew, possessed a mobile telephone, but on the line reserved for such a number, on the front page of his diary, he had written a capital I followed by six asterisks, and suddenly Brett had an inspiration: this was an aide-memoire to his computer password.

Excitedly he turned the computer on, and typed the seven characters in the line under Gordon's name. Immediately the screen cleared, and he was looking at Gordon's desktop. At least now he knew that the mysterious message constituted Gordon's password: how it had appeared was another matter. Nonetheless, he couldn't bring himself to investigate what was shown: instead he hastily closed the computer down and switched off.

The next day he felt better able to explore. Soon the screenful of icons was revealed to him, and he set himself the task of going methodically through them. Some of them were various of Gordon's writings in different stages of completion: Brett had once tried to read one of his books, but given up after just a few pages, admitting to himself that he didn't really understand what Gordon was getting at, so he mentally crossed those off.

Then there were programmes dealing with Gordon's finances, many of which he already knew about through communications from the solicitor. Half-a-dozen folders contained porn images, and at first he wouldn't look at them, closing them immediately it was obvious what were their contents. But a few days later he went through them, telling himself he mustn't shrink from knowing what Gordon had liked.

Some of them were the sort of thing he had expected, nude images of men on their own or with other men. Some of them, though, were rather more shocking: he had heard of fisting, but now here it was on the screen. He wondered what sort of man would let himself be photographed with another man's hand in a place for which Nature had not designed it.

Then there were actual videos of men being penetrated by machines. He was both appalled and fascinated, unable to take his eyes off what was being shown. At least, he reassured himself, Gordon had never, so far as he knew, actually tried any of these things, nor had he ever suggested to Brett that they should experiment in those ways.

But then, tucked away at the bottom of the screen, in what he assumed to be just a calendar, he found details of Gordon's sex-life. There was an index of names and phone-numbers, with comments appended such as 'Big cock, lousy sex' and 'Gives expert blow-job.'

To the best of his knowledge, he hadn't met any of these people, but it was obvious the comments were based on personal experience, and the dates made it clear that Gordon had been going with them right up till a couple of days before his death.

He had always known that Gordon was a strongly sexual person, but their joint sex-life had been both infrequent and, he supposed, somewhat tepid. He hadn't thought much about it, but now he realised that their living together hadn't changed Gordon; he had merely kept that side of his life hidden from Brett.

These revelations preyed on his mind, and eventually he knew he had to talk it over with someone. The obvious person was Carson. He didn't suppose his discoveries would come as any surprise to him: probably Brett was the only person who didn't know what Gordon had got up to, he reflected bitterly.

Carson did indeed immediately admit that he was aware of Gordon's extra-curricular activities. He could see how distressed Brett was, both at finding out what Gordon was really like, and also from feeling that he had failed his lover, and that Gordon ought to have been able to get what he wanted from Brett.

Carson did his best to set Brett's mind at rest, telling him that these sexual encounters meant little or nothing to Gordon: he felt the same way about sex as he did about eating, that it was an appetite that needed to be satisfied. It didn't compare in any way, he assured Brett, with the love they had had for each other. That was too precious to Gordon for him to risk it, since he had known Brett wouldn't understand his addiction to sex, which was why he had kept it secret.

Brett seemed reassured by this, but there was something else worrying him. 'Who do you think showed me the password?' he demanded. 'Was there someone who hated Gordon, or was it someone trying to get their own back on me because of what he left me?'

Carson smiled. 'So far as I know,' he answered, 'Gordon never gave it to anyone. He didn't keep secrets from me, and I'm sure I would have heard if he'd told anyone else.'

Brett was silent for a while, digesting the implications.

At length he looked up and asked uncertainly 'Are you saying he wanted me to know what he'd been doing?'

'That would be my guess,' Carson agreed.

'But why?'

'Perhaps he thought – thinks – that you should have a more realistic picture of him. One thing I'm sure of, he wouldn't want you to behave as if your life was over. He didn't leave you this house for you to turn it into a museum to his memory: it was so that you could enjoy your life when he died. He was over twenty years older than you, remember: he expected you to outlive him.'

There was another period of silence while Brett thought it over, but eventually he said to Carson 'Last time I went out with Tony and Martin, there was a guy who kept looking at me. Do you know if he goes there regularly?'

'There's only one way to find out,' said Carson, rising. He waited till Brett had put a jacket on, and then they went out together.

CLINGING

Gail Morris

The protective plastic split as June helped Rachel manoeuvre the wedding dress into the back of the car, and an escaping fold lapped itself around her wrist.

'What a horrible fabric,' said June.

'Isn't it,' said Rachel. 'Only a het would choose it. And I've had to sew the stuff. But what can you do; I need the money.'

'You want to tout for lesbian weddings, then you'd see some fashion.'

'Would I?' Black serge or washed-out denim is my guess.'

Rachel was to drive the dress across London to her customer in Merton. 'Rather an emergency,' she's explained. 'The infant's due any day, hence the Empire style.'

But June had only just said, 'Merton! Now *that's* a coincidence. I used to know someone there, a sort of ex, actually. In fact, and here's the weird thing, we split years ago but I dreamed of her last week, and yesterday, when I was cleaning out some papers, I found an old letter of hers. Gave me quite a shock actually. Now doesn't that say something to you?'

'Say what?'

'Well it's a kind of message, don't you think. So, as you're going that way you could drop me off, couldn't you? Just a flying visit. Well it *is* nearly Christmas; goodwill and all that.'

Rachel had no objection. The journey through Brixton and Clapham was tedious even on a Sunday and it would be nice to have someone to chat to on the way.

Passing Clapham Common, they reminisced about the good old days of Pride there – 'I'm not calling it Mardi

109

Gras,' stipulated Rachel, 'too absurd when it wasn't even on a Tuesday.'

June exclaimed at all the Asian shops doing brisk business, and wanted to stop off for fruit and veg but Rachel was firm about keeping to her timetable and only allowed her to purchase a pot of cyclamen to take to the ex.

As they came along Meratun Way, June revealed that she was calling upon Liza unannounced. 'Not in the phone book. Of course she's ex-directory, that would be just like her.'

'So she might not even be there?'

'No. I'm doing this on spec.'

'What'll you do if she's out?'

'She might even have moved after all this time,' said June carelessly. 'I'll just tag along with you if there's no answer.'

'I can't invite you into this woman's place. You'll be freezing, waiting in the car.'

'Well, you won't be long, will you. You're just handing the dress over.'

'I've got to fit it.'

'Fit it!' June laughed. 'You said she's about to pop. The less it fits the better, I should think. I can't imagine what possessed her to buy such clingy material.'

At Mantle Avenue June seemed less perky, though she recognised the house at once.

'My God, it's just the same, still that miserable holly in the circle of bricks, and those are the same curtains, I swear. The holly was the grandma's idea – did I tell you, she moved her grandma in with us, temporarily forever. I bet she's still there.'

She hesitated before opening the car door. 'Will you wait till I see?'

Rachel watched her go slowly up the path that was edged with zigzag brickwork. She pressed the bell and looked back at the road. Other houses sported festive wreaths on their doors, but this one had a closed bleak look.

She pressed the bell again, and this time the door opened almost at once to show a small person in a wrap-around overall. Rachel leaned across to wind up the window and heard the old flirty voice trill, 'Junie! Of course I knew you, come in, she'll be made up to see you.'

June directed a shrug and a wave at Rachel and followed the old lady into the dimly-lit passage.

The bride-to-be was very jolly, thrilled with the dress, which she thought both concealed and showed off the bump to perfection. It would make an ideal cocktail frock when she got her figure back, she said; she would dye it lilac. Her mother, well sherried-up with a huge black cat on her knee, grinned in agreement and tried to force a large glass of Emva Cream onto Rachel as she must be tired after her journey. Rachel refused, explaining several times that she had to drive back. The bride said they would definitely send Rachel photos to add to her portfolio. Rachel said that would be lovely, but privately resolved never to admit having made this dress.

'Now, you'd like cash, wouldn't you,' said the bride and proceeded to hunt through the house to make up the amount, opening drawers at random and even snatching up her mother's handbag without as much as a by your leave. Rachel murmured that she would accept a cheque and the mother said, 'I'd take the money, love, if it were me, even if it is a bit short,' and laughed so that the cat wobbling on her lap sank its claws in to retain its place.

It was a relief to get out of there and return to collect June. When she reached Mantle Avenue she realised she didn't know the number, but that it was somewhere towards the middle of the row, and the gardens were very distinctive, which would help. She remembered the little holly tree, but it didn't seem to be there. She drove down to the end, turned back at the roundabout and scrutinised the houses again. Still no little tree and she was nearly at the end of the road, and being hooted at for going too slow. She parked and went back on foot. Lights had come on in porches and windows, some twinkling and colourful. The house must be here somewhere. There was a holly but it was much bigger, not a mere twig, more like a bush. Perhaps the dark made it seem larger. The brickwork, from what she could make out, was the same.

She pushed the bell and there was no sound within. She resorted to the knocker. Still no response. It was getting really cold. She went next door and explained that she could get no answer at number 31.

'No, you won't. It's been empty all year. The agent can't seem to shift it,' said the man in a tone of annoyance. 'I've been cutting the grass and that and I'm getting fed up of it, I can tell you.'

It seemed a slow-motion nightmare after that; calling the police, hanging about for them to find someone with the keys to open the totally empty house, then the repetition of a barrage of questions, as if it were her fault.

The old lady and her grand-daughter had died within a month of each other the previous winter. 'And the joke is,' said the disgruntled neighbour who was now more amenable and chatty, 'they'd both had the flu jab and wanted *me* to have it too. "Not on your nelly," I said, and how right I was.'

At last the police let Rachel go, as it was clear she could tell them nothing more. But they warned they might be in touch at a later date. Rachel tried the patience of her friends for weeks with the story, going over and over what she had heard the old woman say – '"She'll be made up to see you." Isn't that sort of northern? Could she have been northern?'

'As she wasn't *there*, Rachel,' one of them pointed out, 'whatever she was doesn't matter, does it?'

Rachel persisted and eventually satisfied herself with a sort of answer to her puzzle. She was making a suit for an acquaintance of June's who was intrigued, not so much by June's disappearance but by the fact of June's going to see Liza at all.

112

'I absolutely remember June telling me about that affair. Yes, she ended it but it was nothing to do with the old grandmother, though she did say it was a bit much Liza moving the old girl in. Put rather a kybosh on the high jinks. I know June was impulsive, but I thought she's never want to see Liza again at all. At the time what she said to me was, she was well shot of her, she was very dependent, clingy and she was the sort that never lets go.'

THE REFERENCE

Anne Stanesby

She was hard. Everything about her came to a point: her shoes, her nails, her nose and her hairstyle. She used the cruise missile approach in her interview with me. Short, sharp, targeted questions which invited short, sharp, no-nonsense replies. Anything more and one knew the interview would rapidly come to an end.

Question: 'How's your plant i.d.?'
Answer: 'Fine, no problem.'
Question: 'Good. Fast on the p.c.?'
Answer: 'Certainly.'
Question: 'How fast?'
Answer: 'Fast enough.'
Question: 'How's your health?'
Answer: 'Fine, no problem.'
And so on.

A tough cookie indeed. But not tough enough to see through the Polyfilla fix I'd done on my C.V., because I got the job. The position in question being that of a caption writer for P.P.I.C., which stands for Plant and People Imaging Centre. I wanted to work with plants, and this was a start. I won't insult your intelligence by repeating the valedictory drivel which appears on PPIC leaflets. Plants – people – the spiritual experience etc. In plain English, we bought photographs of plants and people from a selected band of photographers. Then we sold them on. It was my job to write the captions to these photos so the punters knew what they were getting. I had been a bit concerned that my plant i.d. would not in fact be up to it, even though the photographers were supposed to tell us what the plants actually were. I needn't have worried. It was all a bit basic.

'Lavender on gravel path – Chelsea.'
'Ivy on checkboard patio – Chelsea.'

That was the plants. As for the people, they were all models, young men and women of all types, sweet little children and cherry-pie grannies.

My target was 200 captions a day. There were other women there, but we didn't get much time to talk. The only sound to be heard was the express rattling of about 20 computer keyboards.

One day I flashed up a slide which didn't look right. I'd met the photographer, Rose, and usually her stuff was spot on. The plants and their surroundings were okay: 'Waterlilies in pond with nymph statuette.' But it was the woman who was wrong. She was middle-aged for a start. We never featured *that* age group. And she had not bothered to dye up the white bits which were clearly starting to invade her otherwise dark wavy hair. Nor was she smiling or even looking cosmic. She was in fact looking rather bad-tempered, and you could see her frown lines. She was dressed in boring creased fawny trousers with, I supposed a vaguely acceptable black caftany thing. But the final killer was – no make-up. I put the slide aside for the botanist, who doubled as a people inspector, to scrutinise. Something just wasn't right.

Pointy, as I called her, asked to see me at break.

'Jemima, why did you reject this slide?'

I told her, 'The woman, not our style, is she?' Hopefully this wasn't her mother.

'There is no woman.'

'Yes there is; you can't miss her.'

'We've all looked. There is no woman.'

There was a pause. I knew better than to protest further. If she said there was no woman, well, fine, there was no woman. Pointy took a deep breath, and then gave me the benefit of her bestest smile.

'Jemima, it's been lovely having you but I'm afraid we're going to have to let you go.'

'But why?'

'You see,' the smile began to go crooked, 'we just don't have space here for people with your type of problem, but I'm sure there are other places where you'd fit in fine.'

'Problem?'

'Yes, you didn't mention it at interview, although I did ask about your health, didn't I?'

She did, and it was true that I had not mentioned my time-outs in the big bins of life. Well, if you tell anyone about that, you'll never get a job, will you? How had she found out? Did it matter? She'd rumbled me and that was that. As I'd lied, I couldn't get her on disability discrimination either.

I did just manage to say 'Any chance of a reference?'

'If anyone contacts us on your behalf, we'll tell the truth.'

I knew what that meant.

There was no one to say goodbye to. It wasn't that sort of a place, but on the way out I did bump into Rose, the photographer, in a hurry as usual.

'Rose, that slide …'

'Which?'

'Pond, water lilies, statue – which nursery was it?'

'Oh, C and C, I think.' She pushed past me and plunged into the office.

C and C stood for Calyx and Corolla. They were a posh outfit in Kent with RHS merit awards coming out of their plant pots.

Shortly after I got home, I got a phone call. It was Rose, in casual mode this time.

'Oh Jemima, hi. Sorry I was so rushed. You asked about a slide, and I'm afraid I misled you. It wasn't a C and C, I'm sure of that, but I can't tell you where it was from, I can't remember, sorry.'

I knew then it was a C and C, and she'd had her ears chewed off for telling me.

116

I expect you're wondering why I didn't leave it at that. Because I was in a jam, that's why. I'd lost a few things along the way, but never my reference. She'd labelled me as someone who saw things that weren't there. I couldn't live with that. It wasn't even true. I had seen that woman: she was there, and I had to prove she existed. I spent the next hour sketching what I remembered of her. Luckily I'm quite good at portraits.

A few days later I put my trusty old bike on a suburban train. C and C were a bit too far away to walk it, and would there be a bus? I thought not. I got there in half an hour and as I cycled past a *pieris* to die for, I felt sure something was up. This type of place is usually crawling with people in springtime, which it was, but not today. Today business was bad. But with all those broken windows and dead-looking plants, was it surprising? It was all very un-C and C.

So I had no trouble spotting her. She was, as it happened, looking with interest at the water lily display. I thought too soon how easy this was turning out to be! As I went forward to meet her, I found myself encircled by a grim-faced band of chaps in green boiler suits embossed with violet ivy-shaped C and C motifs.

'Can we help you, madam?' (said with a sneer.)

'Oh – I'd like to speak to the lady.'

'No ladies working here.'

'Oh, she must be a customer then.'

'No customers here today, only you, if that's what you are.'

'But I saw her in the greenhouse. She's got dark wavy hair and I'd seen her before in a photo of your water lily exhibit at Chelsea.'

They didn't like that a bit. I could have been a foul virus from outer space or a sap-sucking insect or a notifiable disease. The circle started to close in on me.

117

'You'd better get out.'

'Before we call the police.'

'On yer bike – madam.' (said with that self-same sneer.)

Suddenly a gap opened up in the circle and, as intended, I bolted through it, leaving the premises in some haste.

Well, I have to say, I needed a drink after that. In the nearest village, Withycombe, I found a nooky little pub. Luckily the bar person was a human being. Over a pint of strong beer he filled me in with the dirt about C and C.

'Oh, they've had no end of trouble up there. Vandals smashing things up, plants keep dying on them. They got nowhere at Chelsea this year. It's a shame; they were doing fine before. They think it's one of their competitors.'

'But why suspect me?'

'Well, let's face it, love. They know you're not local, and who the hell makes a journey out here to visit a nursery, without a vehicle to take the plants away in. They must have thought you were up to something.'

Well I was, in a way, but I didn't mean them any harm. The beer went straight through me, and soon I had to break off the chat and go to the loo. On the way I peeped out at the garden. It looked nice, a good place to sit in the summer. And then I saw her again. She was out there, and she wasn't angry any more. She smiled at me, and gave a wave as if to say goodbye; then, before I could find the way to go out there, she was gone. Well, this time I would find her, but I'd better have a good story. I thought one up on the loo, always the best place to find inspiration.

I went back to the bar.

'I didn't go there to buy plants,' I told the barman. 'I'm on a different sort of quest. I was looking for a woman, a friend of my mother's. You see my mother died recently after a long illness. She knew there was no hope, and she kept asking me to give this and that memento to one or other of her friends. I did try to write it all down, and I

118

meant to put the notes in a safe place, but well, I'm not very organised, I'm afraid. Mum mentioned a lady who lived here whom she wanted to give something to, and she said they used to visit the C and C nursery. So I went there because I thought they might be able to help. I didn't mean any harm.'

'I don't suppose you know what the lady looked like?'

'All I've got is this sketch. There was someone like this in the nursery and in your back garden.'

He looked embarrassed and shook his head.

'I don't think so, love. It's a good likeness. I'd swear this is Rhona Page who died a few months ago, poor lady. Sorry.'

'Why did you say "poor"?'

'Well, she had a bad road crash, and she was never right after that. Her friend Wendy looked after her till the end. She left the area soon after the death, Wendy did. I'm sorry; it's been a shock, I can tell.'

He was right about that, but wrong about the reason. This woman I kept seeing – she was dead. She didn't exist. What was happening to me? He was still talking.

'Rhona's buried over there by the church in the cemetery, next to the flowering currant. She liked that bush.'

'I'll go and look,' I mumbled, 'at least I can put something on the grave.'

First I saw the *ribes*; it was a white one, quite unusual. And then I saw the statue, the one in the photo. I couldn't mistake it. C and C must have borrowed it to go with their exhibit at Chelsea. What a mean trick! Weren't they making enough? I went right up to it, inspecting it closely. I thought I knew why they'd done it. It really was an exceptional piece, quite lovely. Someone paid an awful lot of lolly for that.

'I'm glad you brought it back,' said a soft male voice. 'Did your conscience get the better of you?'

119

I jumped up. The vicar, standing there in his little dog collar.

'Her friend Wendy put that on her grave. She spent her life savings on it. Rhona would have loved it, I know. She would have been so pleased.'

'She does love it,' I said stiffly. 'And she knows it wasn't me who removed it.'

And with that I left with as much dignity as I could muster.

I remember thinking it was all very well for Rhona Page. She'd got her statue back. C and C must have decided, after my visit, that keeping it was bad news. But I, what had I got now? Things looked bleak for me.

The letter came a few days later, postmarked Kent. The address was a nice-sounding place and the house was called Daisymead.

Dear Ms Stone,

I am writing to ask if you would consider a position down here, helping me care for my garden. It is becoming too much for me, as I am getting on now (aged 82!) I could provide accommodation, and there would be plenty more gardening work available. My late dear friend Miss Rhona Page spoke so warmly of you, I'm sure you'd be just ideal for this job. Will you consider it?

Hoping to hear from you soon.

Yours sincerely, Mrs Sadie Hirst.

Rhona Page had given me the one thing I most wanted, a reference.

MARTIN

Frank Storm

Maureen's quizzical look seemed to indicate that she wanted to be on her own, and Peter obliged by withdrawing to the kitchen. She had insisted on handing over the keys herself on completion day. His solicitor had agreed that it was unusual but not wrong, and Peter had accepted her invitation. After some awkward moments, with tortured conversation, she had handed over the keys and then the look came which sent him out of the room.

When he turned, lighting a cigarette, she was behind him. It startled him and he said: 'I thought you wanted to be alone, say farewell and all that.'

She giggled nervously. 'No,' she replied, 'I wanted to ask you a personal question.'

He braced himself. Any place else he would be evasive, but this was Brighton and one could be out about it here.

'Are you married?' she asked innocently.

'No,' he replied, 'I am gay.'

Her face lit up with relief and she said: 'Good, you'll probably be okay then.' She suddenly became businesslike, told him about refuse collections and where the cheapest shop was. 'Oh,' she said, 'and save your money. Don't change the locks, it won't be of any use.' Then they shook hands and she left, not looking back.

He stubbed out the cigarette and looked out of the window, wondering at Maureen's odd remarks. The sea could just be seen and he savoured the view. After a moment he went into the lounge to start unpacking the tea chests containing his belongings.

Peter had been transferred from his job at American Express in London to the office here in Brighton. Needing to find somewhere to live, he had spotted the advert for this flat in Brighton's local paper. It seemed to be well below the market value, suggesting something must be wrong with it, but he knew it was his kind of apartment as soon as he saw it.

It was a one-bedroom property on the top floor of one of the Regency houses lining the sea front. The views along the coastline were spectacular and it was walking distance from the office. He had immediately offered the asking price, which Maureen had accepted. Things had been remarkably quick by English standards and now, barely two months later, he had actually moved in.

He entered the lounge and stopped in the doorway. There, on one of the chests sat a young man. He was handsome, his tight T-shirt and jeans showing off his swimmer's build. Peter said brusquely: 'Who are you?'

The young man turned around, smiled and said: 'Hello, my name is Martin. I used to live here.'

'Well,' Peter replied, 'this is my house now and I want you to leave and not come back!' He was not normally this rude, but the sudden appearance of this man had profoundly shocked him.

'Why?' asked the young stranger, 'I won't be in the way or any trouble!'

Peter couldn't believe his ears and replied: 'I don't want to share this flat, and certainly not with someone I don't know!'

'Well, we'll get to know each other – I will visit you quite regularly,' Martin replied pleasantly. 'Don't worry, I won't move in nor crowd you and you will be quite safe with me. And when you want me to go, I will!' He stood up, smiled and walked past Peter to the front door, opened it and shut it behind him.

Peter was dumbfounded. Maureen's words came back to him and he wondered if she had meant Martin. He was attractive and very much to his taste, but he definitely didn't want people to use his flat as their home. He made a mental note to have the locks changed despite Maureen's advice. Aggravated, he began to unpack, hang up pictures and arranged the furniture. He worked all day and finally decided he had done enough. He showered and went out for a bite to eat and go to the bars. He had a pleasant evening and actually talked to a few men. At about midnight he returned home.

A light was glowing softly in the lounge and Martin sat on the settee reading a book. Peter's heart jumped, but somehow he liked the young man being there. Martin got up as he entered, complimented him on what he had done to the flat and suggested he made a cup of cocoa, an offer which Peter accepted with a giggle. Later, curled up on the settee, with the hot mug of cocoa in his hand, they chatted. Then his guest suddenly got up, said goodnight and disappeared. 'Odd,' Peter thought, not without some disappointment, as he undressed and slipped into bed.

Maureen had been right. Martin was still waiting for him after a day's work, despite the changed lock, and life went on that way. He would be there after Peter came home from work or from a night out. As promised, he was discreet. If Peter brought someone home, Martin would not be seen anywhere. Only after the night's lover had left would he suddenly appear. Or Peter would sometimes, if the young man brought back stayed overnight, wake up seeing Martin looking at his partner. Then he'd look at Peter, shrug, and leave the flat.

Their relationship began to intensify and Peter found to his astonishment that he stayed in more. He stopped bringing anybody home when he did go out. This was all the more surprising as they never touched. He had no idea what Martin's handshake was like, how his skin felt or whether his full lips were soft or firm. Whenever he moved close to him, Martin would move away or even leave.

One night Peter asked Martin to stay.

'Why?' he responded.

'Well it would be good to get to know each other more intimately, don't you think? After all, it's been a year now!'

Martin went quiet, then murmured: 'You would not want to make love to me.'

'You're wrong there,' Peter said as he moved closer to the other man, but Martin got up and made for the front door. As he opened it he said softly, not looking back: 'You'd die if we made love.'

'Some boast!' Peter scorned.

'No, no boast,' snapped his friend, 'a warning!' and with that he slipped through the open door and disappeared.

Time passed. The incident did not seem to affect their relationship. If anything it intensified, though still without any physical closeness. One night Peter went to an AIDS benefit concert at the Dome and ran into Maureen. He said hello and they talked for a while. Then she asked him how he enjoyed living at the flat. He told her and asked if she had met Martin. Her face clouded over.

'Yes,' she replied, 'he was hateful to me.' She related how he had pestered her, never leaving her flat, being rude to her friends until no one came to visit her any more. And no matter how often she changed the locks, the little rut would always manage to get in, she said. Then she asked how he got on with Martin, and he confessed he wanted nothing more than that they'd become lovers. She looked at him, startled, and paused. Then she took his arm and firmly directed him to the bar.

'Let's have a drink,' she said. 'You'll need one when you hear what I have to tell you.' She ordered a couple of drinks and they went to a table as far away from the milling crowd as possible.

'I kept changing the locks,' she started without preliminaries, 'and finally I'd had as much as I could take. So I went to the police and demanded protection. An officer came out, and went very quiet when we got to the house. Once inside the flat, he told me it had been the place of a very vicious homophobic murder. The owner, someone called Martin – he had forgotten the surname – had been stabbed with a big hunting knife. It seemed the murderer had already killed two other men, always the same way; they took him home, they had sex and then the guy killed them. He did it so quickly it didn't make any noise, and nobody had ever seen or heard anything. The police had filed the case away, since they could not find the criminal, even though there was always a clear set of fingerprints of the culprit on a mug or a glass!'

She paused and looked at him intently, but Peter was unable to return the look. It had irked him that Martin would never allow him to get close, would never touch, let alone kiss him. He had wondered sometimes that his friend might not be flesh and blood, but had dismissed it as too improbable. To have it now confirmed in this way chilled him to the bones. He got up and pushed his way through the throng crowding around the bar in his hurry to get out of the bar and into the fresh air.

He stood there, breathing hard. Maureen had followed him and touched his hand. 'I'm sorry,' she said, 'but I had to tell you when you said you wanted him to be your lover.' He looked at her, then nodded and walked away, going across the road to the Sauna. He stayed there all night, changing men as often as he changed the towels. In the morning he took the train to London and continued his frantic sex spree there. But it didn't help – he could not get Martin out of his head and finally, after four days and nights, he returned.

Martin was waiting behind the door, and the relief on his face when he saw Peter was so touching that the latter broke down sobbing on the floor. Martin joined him and looked at him intensely. 'You look awful,' he said after a while. 'Where have you been?'

Peter smiled through his tears. 'Trying to get away from you,' he replied and went on to explain, in response to Martin's quizzical look, that he had met Maureen.

Martin understood immediately, and held out his hand. 'Take it,' he said. Peter grabbed it, but had to let go with a startled cry, so intense was the cold. 'Now do you believe that you'd die if we made love? And why I always kept away from you?'

'It's academic, don't you agree,' came the reply. 'You're alive and I'm dead.'

'So why are you here?' asked Peter.

Martin averted his eyes and hesitated, then replied soflty: 'To watch over you. Sooner or later you are going to bring that creep back, and I'll be here to make sure he will never be able to hurt anyone again. Then I'll be free to go,' he paused to take a breath, 'if I want to!' He got up and vanished.

It was the one and only time Martin performed that trick. He returned to his tangible form from then on but, as ever, kept a distance between them. Peter felt, though, that a change had taken place, that Martin seemed more reluctant to leave each night. He himself stayed in as usual and only went out occasionally, invariably returning home without a partner. The frantic sex spree after Maureen's revelation had only convinced him that he was better off with Martin, since mentally they were very much alike.

There was another AIDS Benefit night and he went again. Maureen was there too and they greeted each other amicably. When the show started he found a rather nice looking young man sitting in the seat next to him. He was blond, ruggedly handsome, though the mouth and eyes seemed a bit too thin and small. In the interval they started to talk and he found himself inviting the young man, who had told him his name was Jonathan, to have a drink in his flat after the concert.

As they walked home his guest seemed a pleasant enough man, and he began to look forward to what lay ahead. He could do with it too; it was a long time since he had made love. He opened the front door, let in his guest and was startled to see Martin, who had never before been around when he brought someone back. His brown eyes bore coldly into the blond man's back. He closed the door and the young man, who had not seen Martin, followed him into the lounge, sat down and waited for the drinks Peter was preparing in the kitchen.

There was a loud gasp from the hallway. Peter stuck his head round the door to see what was going on. Jonathan stood near the front door that Martin blocked and his guest, white as a ghost and hyperventilating, was trying in vain to get past him. Peter tried to intervene but was roughly pushed aside.

Martin began to move towards Jonathan, who retreated faster and faster until they reached the balcony. Peter could not see how Martin managed it, but suddenly its door was open and they stepped onto it. To Peter's horror the blond drew a big hunting knife from an inside pocket in his jacket and began to slash as Martin, who laughed a loud, lugubrious laugh while still pressing forward.

The rugged blond was forced against the balcony rails and began to cry and whimper, begging for mercy.

'Mercy?' Martin said softly. 'What mercy did you have for me or the others when you killed us?' With that he pushed his murderer, who wailed at his touch, till he fell over the railing onto the pavement below. The silence that followed was broken only by Martin's hard, rasping breath.

'You said you would be free to go after you had dealt with your murderer,' Peter finally said softly. 'Does that mean that now you're going to leave me, and I'll never see you again?'

'You are alive, young, good-looking,' came the reply. 'You should be with your own kind. You should live!'

'I do, when I'm with you!' Peter said simply. After a long pause in which their eyes never lost contact he continued: 'Can't you stay?'

Martin sighed and sat down, then finally said: 'If you really want me to!'

'I do,' Peter replied.

'Whatever you say,' Peter mumbled.

He went to the phone to call the police, reported the incident. Amongst the officers that came was the sergeant

127

who had investigated the previous murder. He saw Martin as soon as he entered, blanched and had to steady himself against the wall. While the officers, who seemed unaware of Martin's presence, questioned Peter the sergeant went to the balcony and meticulously searched it. Satisfied with what he saw there, he turned and looked at Martin. For a moment their eyes locked, then the sergeant told his men all was clear and thanked Peter for his co-operation.

When the police had left, Peter phoned his parents to tell them the story and say good-bye, after which he went to Martin, bent over and kissed his icy lips. 'Come,' he said. Martin began to protest, but Peter said: 'Just come,' took his hand and led him into the bedroom.

The flat was sold soon after. Peter's parents had driven down immediately after the call, but by the time they had arrived he was already dead. He and Martin watched, hand in hand, as his parents washed him. Then both lovers turned and disappeared without looking back.

BRIEF ENCOUNTER

Elsa Wallace

'She's a bit pathetic in bed,' said Lucy casually, as though she might say Shirley was a useless cook. 'Past it, I suppose. She's at least 53, maybe more.'

'And that's why you're passing her on to me?' said Carol.

'I'm *not* passing her on. You just meet her, have supper, explain things. I can't do it. You're supposed to be a mate.'

'There's mates and mates. This is a bit off. Why don't you just phone her?'

'I *told* you, I can't stand to hear her voice – it's all – ugh, tasteless is all I can say. I can't go through with it. I hate endings, you know how I am. They're gruesome. You'll be okay with her, just explain, like, I've gone away, urgently called away, I would have phoned but it all happened very sudden.'

'You've gone away, sudden, and simultaneously gone off her: isn't that going to sound strange?'

'Well, it *is* strange, I don't deny it. I didn't expect this to happen. When I met Gina I never thought of it but whammo, it's like there's never been anyone else. Don't say it's never happened to you.'

'Not when I'm in the middle of an affair with someone else.'

Lucy wriggled. 'Well, I wouldn't really call it an affair. Just a sort of … relationship, I suppose.'

Carol laughed. 'Relationship! That's a nice jargon word.'

'Well, a kind of, you know, short-lived attraction then. It was always an on–off thing.'

'If that's all it was you can break it off, can't you? Oh no … I see … it means more to her, is that it?'

'I don't know. She's sort of laid back, too. She wasn't always straight with me, you know. I know she has her own life. I wasn't always part of it. I bet she still shags her husband.'

'But you are enough a part of her life – she's given you enough prezzies.' Carol was unable to bite back a twinge of envy at the prezzies.

Lucy rattled her bangles. 'Oh, prezzies! I gave her stuff too. Anyway, why are we discussing this. Look, what's the prob? She's not violent.'

'I should hope not.'

'She's cool, sophisticated. You know, you've met her.'

'That only makes it worse. I really don't see why I should do this.'

'You're the bloody actress. You can carry it off. Act apologetic, embarrassed.'

'I won't be acting. It *is* embarrassing.'

'No, it's not; well, not for you. It's like, civilised.'

'What?'

'I could leave her a note but that's so cold. I do feel something for her. She should be let down gently. And you can do that. You've done it often enough for yourself.'

Carol scowled. It was true but one didn't want to hear it.

'The rooms are booked and paid for, it's all arranged. You only have to show up, introduce yourself – she may have forgotten you, she's not good on faces – have the meal, do the bizz. It's all paid for but here's some extra for tips or whatever.'

'Whatever?'

'You might like some bubbly … I don't know.'

'This is my expenses, is it?'

'In a way. If you like.'

'I don't like, Lucy. I really don't like this at all.'

'But you *will* do it? Please, Carol. I'm *desperate*. Just this once. I'll never ask again.'

'You'd better not, my flighty friend.'

Lucy grinned in relief, the grin saying 'good old Carol, always dependable.'

Carol had known perfectly well all along that she would do it. Getting Lucy out of her scrapes was a permanent feature of their friendship. Friendship, is that what you call it, she mocked herself. They had known each other too long but she was always diverted by Lucy's quicksilver nature. It was flattering to be the only friend who had stood the test of time. She realised this might not have been so if Lucy had been very plain. She was adorable, a modern Dora Spenlow, from her eight-year-old giggly self to the little blossom adult with her clear skin and eyes, soft brown hair, her boundless enthusiasm in living, her short-lived fancies, her humour – they'd called her Tee-Hee at school – her teasing and cajoling.

She seemed guileless, she always meant well, she was generous and loving. But, Carol knew, it was better to be a friend to Lucy than a partner. She ran through life and there were always other flowers and butterflies to amuse her. When you thought about it she wasn't even as practical as Dora, who had after all looked after her pet dog Gyp. Carol had been the recipient of several rabbits Lucy had tired of: 'Oh, do take him, Carol, he likes *you!*'

And now she was to break it to Shirley that she was to be re-homed, as it were. Did other people do this for their girlfriends? Carol, between jobs, wondered if this were a niche in the lesbian market. Could she earn a few quid taking out other women's cast-offs and breaking the news gently? Lucy's coming out was for her just another of the pleasant little japes life offered. It was a merry little secret kept from her parents.

She took it for granted that Carol also was lesbian. Though so different, their sharing of this didn't strike her as a startling coincidence. It was as if they both got the same gift off the Christmas tree. In fact, thought Carol, life was still some sort of toyshop to Lucy, and perhaps that wasn't strange. Her mother had been 50 when pregnant with this

131

afterthought child. This lastborn remained their babykins, indulged but somehow not entirely spoiled. Lucy retained her original infant cheeriness. She was able to go on dates and yet still played with her dolls at fifteen. To please her parents she went out with suitable boys, sons of their friends and colleagues, but was always able to detect a flaw which made them unmarriageable.

'He's got a funny smell, Mummy,' she would say blandly, or 'His hands feel sticky.' To Carol she said 'Marriage must be ghastly. Imagine, you could have a baby boy and then you wouldn't be able to dress it up.'

Sometimes Carol thought uneasily that there was a shadow of Childie about Lucy and hoped she wasn't turning into Sister George herself. But she was fairly sure she wasn't attracted sexually to Lucy. It was just that Lucy had always been there: she was the link with childhood, with school, with the old home, her own parents, she was the sister she had never had. Actually she was glad she hadn't had a real sister. Invidious comparisons were bound to have been made. As it was, her mother had commented 'It's a pity you can't be more like Lucy, she's so dainty.' Her mother had no idea of the coarse jokes Lucy could repeat at the drop of a hat; my 'lorry driver jokes' as she called them.

Sitting in the hotel lounge, Carol wondered how long Lucy would go on being Lucy. Perhaps the whole girlikins act was protective mimicry and there was another Lucy under there somewhere. Would she eventually fulfil that potential or would she be what Dickens described as a young lady of 60? Of course people didn't age so rapidly nowadays. Lucy's ex, for example, was in her fifties but looked more like thirties, for all Lucy's disparaging remarks now that the new treat was on her plate. Shirley was a smart businesswoman, admittedly with a husband and family in tow, but in charge of her own life.

Nine o'clock came and went and Carol relaxed. After coffee she would go to the desk and say she was going up to bed, and would they let her cousin Mrs Fairley know, if she did arrive after all. Shirley should have been there at six. There was no message, so Carol was pleased to assume she wasn't coming. And I'm not going through this again, she decided. If need be I'll write the blasted letter for Lucy but I'm not doing the person-to-person stuff. This is a supper too far.

She was booked in under Lucy's name and it had seemed peculiar taking the key for Ms Linton. What had the relationship with Shirley been like? All she knew was that the pair of them had these hotel rendezvous on a fairly regular basis. Lucy had only said that it was good fun, and she would dwell on the menus and service rather than what she and Shirley got up to.

Except once, when excitedly she reported 'Shirley's got a new emerald green negligée, fantastic, and she was sitting at my dressing table and she gave me this special smile. My knees are still melting!'

But was one to take this seriously when it was followed by the tee-hee giggles of old and then a serious recommendation of the hotel – 'the starters are fabulous, you should take Tricia there.'

'No, I shouldn't,' Carol had retorted, 'we can do what we do at home.'

She had always been a bit mean. And she didn't have Lucy's fondness for hotels; Lucy had confessed they were rather a fetish with her, and sex was better in them – 'deliciously creepy' was how she put it. 'I just love the anonymity, and the staff always look a bit odd, and you think how many people have slept in the bed before you, and it's all sort of impersonal, like being on a film set.'

Perhaps Lucy should have been the actress. She made you laugh, she was quite a good mimic. Her parents had hoped for a singing career for her but she was content to trill in the chorus of amateur shows or sometimes at weddings. Otherwise her time was spent in her uncle's bookshop and gallery where she 'filled in' as she called it.

133

Carol didn't enquire into Lucy's finances, but assumed there were hefty top-ups to her salary from her parents, hence the indulgence in hotels. She and Shirley would book in separately for these rendezvous, pretending to be cousins. The make-believe was all part of the fun, as much as the sneaking into each other's rooms, apparently. All because Lucy at fourteen had once stayed alone in a hotel – the frisson of adventure from that occasion seemed to never have quite evaporated.

Carol supposed the hotels were chosen with care; Shirley's husband wasn't to learn of the liaison. 'But of course there's always the risk,' said Lucy, eyes shining, 'his colleagues might bob up anywhere.'

The flotsam and jetsam in this hotel were sparse, perhaps this was a bad night. Carol had her meal, a run-of-the-mill pasta dish with dubious veg, drank as much as felt safe and poodled off to bed to rehearse what to say when Shirley popped her head round the door: 'Oh hi, d'you remember me? Lucy's old school chum? She can't make it tonight. Or any night, it seems.'

Perhaps it would be a good ploy to sound irritated and put-upon, they could be tetchy together, share their gripes about Lucy, have some more vodka (the mini-bar was rather good) and have a bit of a laugh.

This prospect cheered her up somewhat. The décor of the room was not too soulless. The bland prints on the wall opposite the bed showed views of the Thames.

The mattress was sleepable. Carol put on her pyjamas and watched TV with the sound off – she liked studying body language in this way. She woke later to what seemed to be a porn movie. A semi-nude woman sat in a bedroom smiling seductively over her shoulder. Then Carol saw, in the subdued light, that a woman sat at her own dressing table, smiling at her in the mirror. She wore green lace.

Carol gaped. The woman put her finger to her lips, still seeming to smile. Carol shut her eyes hard and re-opened them. The woman was still there. She had risen and

134

switched off the TV and Carol felt rather than saw her approach the bed. She slid under the covers in a smooth practised way, hardly disturbing the sheets. Her face and hands were pleasantly cool. She smelled of spices and rose fragrance.

Carol wanted to say 'I'm not Lucy' ridiculous as that was, for they were nothing alike. Shirley's touch was gentle and assured and Carol sank back under it. There was a faint vibration of distant music that seemed to make speech unnecessary. She realised regretfully that she had drunk too much to make the most of what was happening.

Shirley was gone before Carol woke to a thumping headache. She couldn't eat the paid-for breakfast. A mini-bar is a dangerous toy, she realised, shocked at the amount she had drunk. But then she remembered that Shirley could have knocked back some of it. She thought she could associate the taste of sherry, or was it brandy, with her.

After such a night she didn't feel inclined to go back to her flat. With enough of Lucy's expenses in hand, she took herself shopping, got aspirin, some badly needed tights, and jaunty earrings, after which she felt recovered enough for a light lunch in a nice little café.

By the time she reached home, the answerphone was buzzing with Lucy's increasingly anguished messages: 'Carol, if you're there, will you please bloody pick up?'

She did so, to be met with a barrage of 'Where the hell have you been? I've been ringing for hours.'

'I've been looking for a job,' returned Carol sharply; she sometimes said this to emphasise the precariousness of her existence compared with Lucy's silver-spooned life.

'Oh. Well, I need you, *desperately*, you must come round. NOW. It's all too horrible.'

She did sound distressed; Carol could almost feel the little paws clutching her arm. Shirley, she revealed, had been injured in a smash only two minutes from her home, would you believe it, was in hospital with whiplash or something and expected Lucy to visit her this very evening.

'And that's not the worst part,' Lucy squeaked. 'Her husband phoned me, Gervase, ugh! I had to speak to him. He knows about us, it's too gruesome. He's being understanding and all that. He'll be there. She expects me to come and see her with *him there*, can you credit it?'

'But why does she want to see you at all?'

'Oh, don't be idiotic. She thinks it's still on with us, of course.'

'Why would she think that?'

'Are you drunk? What else should she think? She still knows nothing, seeing she didn't make the hotel. *I* haven't been in touch with her. She was in Casualty all night. He phoned me lunch time. It really is the pits, my work number and all!'

'Work number,' thought Carol later; 'more like swanning around and swigging Volvic number.'

When the hairs on the back of her neck had subsided, she agreed to accompany Lucy on the frightful bedside visit. Whatever it was that had occurred the previous night, it would be interesting to see if Shirley was wearing the green negligée.

A JOURNEY ROUND THE CIRCLE LINE

Jeffrey Doorn

It all comes back into focus somewhere between Notting Hill Gate and High Street Kensington. I look around and see I'm still here, sitting in the same underground carriage hurtling through a dark tunnel. Even before the deceleration and first flash-by appearance of the station sign on the tunnel wall, I know. A darting look to my left confirms Julian is no longer with me.

All right, I've blacked out and gone past our stop. Julian might have gone thinking I was right behind him. Or perhaps he thought I was faking, and decided to turn the joke back on me. No big deal, I can simply get out here, go round to the other platform and take the first train going the opposite direction.

No, it isn't so simple. Somehow I can't do it. Well, I'll stay on, complete a circuit. Let Julian wait a while; the joke will be twice as piquant.

What a pair, always larking about, never taking anything seriously. That's what brought us together, having the same quirky sense of humour. From our first meeting, at that midsummer party, we just clicked. Sexual chemistry was there too, of course, but what really started the relationship wasn't lust, but laughter. We left the party together, and found ourselves heading for the same bus. I had one of those passes with which you could take a friend for free on weekends, so when we found a seat I took it out. Before I could speak, he whipped his out, shouting 'Snap!' The conductor must have thought us barmy, pointing passes at each other like duelling pistols and collapsing in hysterics.

Our hilarity continued for the rest of the ride; but after he'd gone, I realised I hadn't asked for his number. Next day I phoned our host, ostensibly to thank him for a fun party, but really to ask if he'd give me Julian's number. 'Glad to, but you'd better be quick; he's just rung to ask for yours.'

After that we were inseparable; whether just the two of us, in company with friends, or out among strangers, we were continually nudging each other, commenting on everything and everyone, or simply looking at each other and rolling our eyes. Our remarks may have been a touch bitchy on occasion, with a slightly caustic edge, but we were never vicious or cruel. We even laughed in bed – before or afterwards that is, not during.

We'd been together about six months when he was given the opportunity to take a lease on a tiny bedsit flat in Bayswater. Before he finished asking if I'd share it, I said 'Yes, please.' A few weeks later we moved in. It was in one of those five storey mansion blocks, all white stucco, Ionic pillars flanking the door, stone balustrade out front, first floor balconies with pedimented windows, window boxes on the second and third stories, unadorned windows at top. To me it was heaven.

The rent was a lot more than either of us had been paying before; but it was so central, convenient and cosmopolitan, I didn't care how much it cost. True, my lowly clerical post did not pay much, about £180 a month, but there were always openings in the firm; and being in Personnel, I was among the first to know about staff vacancies. It wasn't a bad place to work, either: bright modern office, good canteen, sports and social club. Most of my colleagues were nice and friendly; as for the others, well, I could take the Mickey out of them when I got home.

Life was sweet. Julian and I went clubbing, saw films, trawled junk shops and flea markets for unusual things to decorate the flat. If we couldn't afford a holiday, Kensington Gardens or Hyde Park were just a short stroll away. Our first summer in Bayswater was hot and sunny, and seemed to go on forever. The next was even hotter, all the grass in the parks burning yellow-brown. We went rowing on the Serpentine, though so ineptly I don't know how we managed to stay afloat. Everything was an adventure, even a long walk to the V&A to giggle at plaster casts of classical statues, or into the Natural History Museum to make faces at the fish and fowl, or dally with the dinosaurs. I'd think of Ogden Nash's lines about a fossil that 'winked, it's kinda fun to be extinct'.

This summer has been dreadful. Poor Queen having her Jubilee – what a washout! Still, we had a few laughs on the carpeted special buses, ludicrously painted silver – distinctly unsuitable when skies are almost always grey. We even braved the showers to watch the Jubilee Day procession, and later the Thames pageant and fireworks.

Last week was Trooping the Colour and next week is Gay Pride; but this weekend we had no plans. I was a bit on edge, having been kept awake by violent thunderstorms, and then facing an interview for an admin job in the department on Tuesday. I was reasonably confident; but by Saturday I needed some distraction.

The morning was overcast and cold, so we stayed in with the gas fire on full – on June 18th! Over lunch we talked about the future. Julian's doing well organising apprentice training; but he's thinking of putting in for a transfer to his company's computer centre. He has ideas about developing computing courses for the staff. If that leads to promotion and I get my job, we're going to try to lease the next door flat when it comes up. There's a wall panel we're sure conceals a connecting door.

With the afternoon slipping away, we decided to go out, but couldn't think what to do. 'Have you ever gone round the Circle Line?'

'What, all the way around? No.'

It seemed a strange way to spend an afternoon, but then we hardly ever used the tube. I took the Number 15 bus to work, and Julian used the 12 or 88 to his training centre, or to meet me in the West End for evenings out.

We ambled along Porchester Gardens, and sashayed down Queensway to Bayswater tube station. I love walking up Queensway every day. So appropriate to have a street for queens. If only we lived in Queen's Gardens, just a few steps from our house, my joy would be doubled.

'Which way: clockwise via Paddington or anti-clockwise via South Ken?'

'Doesn't really matter; we'll just get the cheapest ticket and make a full circuit, then get off one stop beyond Bayswater.'

'Well, I'd rather walk back from Notting Hill Gate than Paddington, so let's go that way.'

What is a journey? For most people it is a means of getting from A to B. For us it was an end in itself. We began this journey in high spirits, observing our fellow passengers and speculating about their lives.

'Those two have been out shopping. She's pleased with their purchases; he isn't so sure.'

'Look at that woman smiling; you think she's just been with her lover?'

'I'll bet that pair are house-hunting. Yes, he's checking the address, she's armed with the A–Z. Notting Hill Gate: One down, 26 stops to go; well, 27, including this one again.'

'Ooh, another gay couple; shall we yell "cooie"?'

'No, don't embarrass them … oh, they've noticed us, they're smiling; aren't they sweet!'

'Oh dear, look at that straight couple, no, over there, the gloomy twosome who just got on.'

'What miserable expressions – must have had a row. See how they're sitting, angled away from each other, not talking … folded arms, set faces – looks serious.'

'Julian, that Indian boy, do you think he's gay? He keeps looking over.'

'Mmm, he fancies you.'

140

'No, it's you; oh, how shy, averts his eyes whenever you glance across.'

'Shall we ask him to join us? Take him home?'

'What a shame, he's leaving. Let's see if he looks back. Wait … yes. Nice smile.'

And so it went on. Families, tourists, Sloane Rangers, culture vultures, shabby genteels, tarty types and glamour pusses – all scurrying to afternoon assignations, getting ready for early evening dates or heading home to prepare dinner. We were not coming from or going anywhere, simply mooching around beneath the cities of Westminster and London for the sake of the ride.

I think they got on at Moorgate. I'd had a dread of that station ever since the disaster, some two and a half years before, when over forty people lost their lives. But I hardly noticed who was boarding; Julian and I were too busy assessing the crowd from Liverpool Street. It wasn't until we'd passed Barbican that their gruff voices caused me to glance across. I immediately turned to Julian.

'Ugh, they look rough.'

'Who?'

'Those three across the aisle.'

'Don't look at them.'

By this time we had pulled away from Farringdon and were heading for Kings Cross, where a crowd piled on. When they filtered out, I shot a wary peek across and quickly looked down at the floor. They were still there; a sour-looking, lanky youth of about 19 in between two slightly younger ones, rather shorter and dumpier.

'Oi, what you lookin' at?' The grating voice cut across the carriage. 'Couple of queers, in't they?' I kept my eyes glued to the floor, hoping if I ignored them, they'd stop.

'Hey, poofter, I'm talkin' to you' They were coming over; three pairs of legs stood right in front of us. 'What you bloody looking at?' I knew the drill; if I said I wasn't, he'd say I was calling him a liar. 'ANSWER ME!'

'What do you mean?'

'Don't play stupid, you fucking pansy.' The one on his right chimed in, 'Makes you sick, dunnit,' the other snarled 'Disgustin'.' I looked around, desperately searching for help from our fellow passengers; but everyone's head was buried in a book or newspaper, or staring ahead. We were coming into Baker Street; Julian rose, his voice slightly shaking, 'Excuse me, we're getting out here.'

'You're not going nowhere.' An arm shot past my head, spatulate fingers bore down on Julian's left shoulder, pushing him back in his seat, just as the doors opened. Several people bolted off; those entering quickly moved away.

'Please,' I begged, 'let us go.' He looked at me with cold eyes, his ugly face made more hideous by a sneering twist of the mouth.

'Nah.'

I took a breath, wanting to shout 'Call the guard, pull the alarm;' but before I could utter a sound, a callused hand was at my throat. A rasping whisper sent rank breath into my face. 'You yell for help and it'll be your last.' The doors had closed; the train lurched ahead.

'Leave us alone,' Julian pleaded, 'we're not hurting you.' The hand left my throat and grabbed Julian. 'Shut up, freak.' I felt a punch on my right shoulder and a kick in the shin, while I saw Julian getting the same treatment from the other side. The ringleader twisted Julian's shirt in his fingers and must have caught the skin, as Julian let out a gasp of pain.

'Stop,' I cried, reaching over to push the hateful arm away from my lover.

'Don't touch me, you fucking poof cunt.'

The flash of a knife. A scream. Sound of doors opening and scramble of boots. Babble of voices. 'Scarper!' 'Get out of it.' 'Stop them.' 'Help!' Julian's face in front of me, his wide eyes looking into mine, his lips forming words as everything blurs. A confusion of sounds, movement,

142

descending into darkness, sounds more distant, fading. Silence.

Out of a cloud, to find myself sitting in a moving underground train. It is slowing down. Coming into High Street Kensington. I don't want this stop, do I? Hasn't this happened before? Where is Julian? I want to go home.

Try to think clearly and work out what is happening. We set out in the afternoon, but as the train goes through South Kensington it appears to be twilight. Calm down, now, be logical. I'm supposed to make a journey round the Circle Line, but seem to keep falling asleep, missing several stops. Well, try to stay awake this time. I feel fine until Moorgate, when I start getting anxious. For the next few stops a growing fear, which builds to terror as we approach Edgware Road ...

It's happened again. Not sleep, more like a faint, and then we're pulling into High Street Ken. Wait a minute, I still have a bus pass, don't I? There are at least four buses I can choose from to get home from here. I stand at the doors as they open, but am immobilised until after they've closed.

We go round again and again. In my trepidation, at Farringdon I peer out and see it's morning. The tube doesn't run all night; did I cut out when it stopped? I can tell the time of day when we emerge above ground, again at South Ken – Sunday afternoon. Families going to museums, just like Julian and I ... Take me with you. I could sail up Exhibition Road, float across the park and be home. Julian must be frantic with worry.

Around and around. Women in smart outfits, men in suits. Briefcases – must be Monday morning. There's Bob, that graduate trainee from the Secretary's Department. One of my rivals for that job. Well, he may have a degree, but I have a couple of years' experience. He's getting out at Mansion House. I'd better follow; I'll be late for work. What's happened? Everyone pushed past me and I couldn't get through to the doors.

The journey continues, over and over; I hardly take note of anyone until I see a couple of girls I recognise from Accounts getting on at Mansion House. Can't quite make out what they're talking about; one says something like 'Couldn't believe it when I heard it' the other nodding and saying 'Tragic, just tragic.' Don't know them well enough to go over, and they haven't noticed me. By the time I've summoned up courage to speak, we've reached Liverpool Street, and they're gone.

I seem to be locked in an inexorable situation, and cannot break the pattern. If only I could somehow transfer to the Central Line and get to Queensway. I start to look forward to certain stations and discernible times, like South Ken at night, when people enter my carriage clutching Prom programmes, talking excitedly about the concert they've just heard. I'm aware all the time, except for those few stations I always miss, and from the end of the last journey of the day until it starts up again next morning.

Saturday comes: no commuter rush hour. Quite a few queens getting on; lots of lesbians too. Of course, it's Gay Pride. I look in vain for Julian. When they all pile off at Temple, I try to get swept off with the crowd, though I know it's impossible. And I so much wanted to join the march this year.

Another week goes. One morning I spot Bob again. He's wearing new shoes. I feel trapped on the wheel of fortune: 'Round and round she goes, where she stops nobody knows.' Raincoats appearing, scarves, gloves, overcoats. The tube map has been altered; looks like the extension to Heathrow has opened as planned. Now revellers getting on – it's a new year.

One night, must be Spring, no more overcoats, it's the last round, only one youngish man at the other end of the carriage. A second man gets on, sits opposite him. They cruise; soon they're hard at it, their short, fervent session finishing just as we pull into another station. They do themselves up quickly and separate, one smearing spilt semen with his shoe, like a dog covering his traces. I watch all this with curiously detached interest, like a critic viewing a porno film. I keep thinking about the sperm crushed into the floorboards.

I find myself taking less and less notice of people as individuals: after a while they're all the same. I do recognise a few regulars, like the pale young man looking rather nervous and uncomfortable in his suit and tie, later seeming more confident. For weeks he's a bright spot in my day. One morning he fails to appear. I resign myself to his absence and forget him. The following week he reappears, sporting a sun-tan. After a while I begin to lose interest. In a few months he's vanished.

It's curious; when the carriage is fairly empty, no one tries to sit in my seat. Often someone will approach, hesitate a moment, shudder slightly and move on. During rush hours or other busy times, I move off to the side, but anyone who sits there reacts in some way, as if sensing something unpleasant. I observe all this impassively. In fact, I avoid people as much as possible, never touch anyone; even when the train is packed, I find a space where I am not in contact.

People are now no more to me than gauges of the change in season or fashion. Sometimes I find myself coming to, after an unexpected loss of consciousness, to find changes in the carriage – new advertisements, for instance, or even fresh upholstery. I assume the train has been in a depot for repair and maintenance, or complete overhaul; but I'm aware of nothing until we're moving again. Don't know which is worse: the dreamless state of suspended animation, or the jolting return to this purgatorial existence. I often wonder whether things would have been different had we opted to go clockwise when this journey began. Perhaps I should not be continually hurtling backwards while the world above goes on without me.

Though the terror abates each time I go around, modifying to dull nausea and resignation, it's the unrelenting monotony that gets me. The boredom. I've counted the grooves in the wooden floors, the number of screws on the raised portion of each panel, the yellow oblongs in the patchwork pattern of the seat upholstery, then the orange, brown and black. Then I've added, subtracted, multiplied and divided them, attempting to establish a predictable sequence – though you'd think I was utterly fed up with predictable sequences.

Despite my waning interest in the world, I've kept up with some events, those in headlines I read across the carriage, or on pages of discarded newspapers facing up on nearby seats. A woman prime minister; I'd have preferred that nice Shirley Williams. A number of royal marriages, almost as many royal divorces, flood, fire, earthquake, hurricane, wars with the most unexpected enemies: Argentina, Iraq – it all seems so remote.

Sometimes events spill into my carriage; then I take more interest, though purely as an observer. Gay gatherings seem to have grown. Good to see queens are still queens, whatever they're wearing: black one year, white another, though I don't know how I feel about that emaciated skinhead look. Some of those boys don't look at all well. I often see that twisty red ribbon. Signal or symbol? When a crowd of gay men and women are riding to Pride or whatever, I search the faces, but never see anyone I know. Once, when they're all piling off at Victoria, I try to attach myself to the backpack of a particularly cute lad; not that I especially fancy him, or want any longer to join the festivities, more out of curiosity to see what Pride events are like now. Of course it's useless.

Most of the time I become aware of fads or innovations as if they were occurring on another planet. What first appears a profusion of transistor radios proves to be portable telephones; when not clamped to their ears, users hold them in their laps, fiddling with them. Also, for a time, I wonder whether half the population are into amateur sports and the other half in the military reserve, judging from what they're wearing.

One day the carriage fills with flowers. Apparently for the Princess of Wales. I've seen her picture so often on papers and magazines. Lady Di, Princess Di, Divorced Di, Dodi's Di; now she's Dead Di. The flowers are pretty, a riot of colour; but something's missing. Yes, that's it – aroma, fragrance; when did I lose my sense of smell? Never realised it until now. Just as well, I suppose. That reminds me, I often see people eating chocolates or whatever, and never feel envy or hunger. Another loss I don't miss.

Proms over – very subdued last night audience going home. Another Autumn. I'm in my usual state of post-Moorgate uneasiness when two men get on at Kings Cross. 'Why are you so uncomfortable?' one asks as they pass.

'You know I never take the underground; I can't bear it – especially this line!' That voice. I look up as they're taking their seats.

'I know,' the other answers; 'but with Thameslink out of action there's no other way. Look, we'll change at Baker Street to the Jubilee Line, and be home in no time.'

'All right; but it's agony being here.' Cautiously I approach them. So often I've imagined I've seen Julian, but it's always an illusion, just someone with a similar build or stance. The other speaks again. 'That was so long ago, Jul, you have to let it go.' Jul? And he's giving his leg a surreptitious little squeeze. Who is he? Don't recognise him. No one we knew. But Julian, yes, it's unmistakable. Oh, he's filled out a bit, has a few character lines, and his hair's starting to grey a bit at the temples – very distinguished. I'm standing directly in front of him. He stirs a little in his seat.

'What is it?' his friend asks.

'I don't know. A sudden chill.'

'Probably a quirk in the ventilation system. Want to change places?'

'No, it's all right.'

147

I reach out to caress Julian's cheek. His eyes widen and dart about. Slowly he raises his hand, placing it over mine; I remember how warm his hands always felt. His friend asks 'Are you all right?'

'Yes, fine.' He breathes deeply 'There's a curious aroma; can you smell it?'

'No. Oh yes, like after rain. Ozone.' He gives a little shrug and turns away. Julian's head tilts back and I'm looking into those eyes. I move closer, meeting his lips in a kiss which, even if neither of us feels, must communicate something. He makes a sound, not exactly a sigh, more like the little signal of pleasure he used to give when I'd brush or lick his nipples, or fondle him in a way he specially liked.

'Okay, Baker Street,' the other voice breaks in, 'let's go.' They stand, collecting their things. I'm face to face with my lover, who seems to be looking at me the way he did the last time I saw him. Now he looks right through me. I turn as the doors open. The other goes first, but Julian turns in the doorway and looks, as it were, straight at me. I believe, yes I'm sure, his lips form my name.

Should I follow him? Is he the key that will release me from this inner circle of hell? I start to move towards him; but he has already turned and gone through the open doors, which slide shut as I get to them. Through the glass I see him catching up with the other man.

Well, I'm glad he's found someone. I hope they're happy together. It was foolish of me to think he'd wait for me forever, or even that he'd go on living in Bayswater. But of course that means I no longer have any home to go to; there's no place for me on earth, no reason to continue this journey. Surely now I can be released.

Before the train reaches Edgware Road all goes black – but next thing I know it's clearing … oh hell, the same loss, the same reawakening. What else must I confront; what else do I have to learn?

Excited crowds celebrating New Year with increasing frenzy as they approach and enter a new century, the word millennium on everybody's lips. How many millennia am I condemned to follow this endless, pointless non-existence? More disasters. Another war. Russia's become our ally?

Now a new excuse for people to celebrate. The Queen is having another Jubilee. I wonder if they're painting the buses gold this time? Signs say the tubes will run all through Jubilee night to get revellers safely to and from fireworks and parties. That's all I need; no rest for the weary.

But even these revels soon are ended. Summer fades; the season of mists begins – but where is my mellow fruitfulness? What can I hope to harvest? I see from a newspaper, left behind by a commuter, that it is Thursday, October 31st. Sure enough, some folks in costume as witches, wizards and the like ride off to Halloween parties. How would they feel if they knew there was a real ghost in their midst? Perhaps I should try to materialise, give them a fright. It would probably require a huge effort – why bother? They go their way, blissfully unaware of me.

This should really be my night. It is high time. I've just worked out I've been down here exactly as long as … why am I still blocking the thought? Face up to it: I've been dead as long as I was alive. Twenty-five years, three months, thirteen days. Here it is, the last train of the night. Few people in the carriage, twelve to be precise. A woman gets off at Moorgate and two men get on – they make crude, suggestive remarks after her and she hurries away.

There's something eerily familiar about one of their voices. Without looking, I'm aware of their flopping into seats opposite me, bantering about the woman's body, and what they'd like to do to her. I'm repelled and terrified as I hear the grating voice I can now place unmistakably. I look across. Two middle-aged, pot-bellied blokes, one utterly nondescript, but the other! With thinning hair, twisted mouth and sagging jowls, he's the same lanky youth gone to seed. He speaks again, inane babble interspersed with swear words, foul language for a foul creature.

Why am I cowering in fear? He can't hurt me now. He's done his worst. Without thinking what I am doing I am up, confronting him with all the pent-up rage of a quarter of a century. *Killer, Murderer,* I shriek, beating him about the head and chest. He shifts in his seat and zips his jacket up. Though my punches do not connect, I'm encouraged by his growing unease. *Bastard, you took my life.* He's shivering now.

'All right, mate?'

'Bloody cold in here.'

'You must be caught in a draught; let's move over there.' They cross the aisle; I step aside, let my hot anger abate, turn to something colder, harder. The killer sits in my seat, but immediately jumps up. 'Shit, it's damp, like someone's been pissin' hisself.'

'Over here, then.' They move again. Some passengers are shooting sidelong glances. Go on, I think, move as many times as you like, you won't escape me. I stand over him, concentrating my cold fury. *You pathetic excuse for a human being, how dare you go on living your putrid life! That's right: shiver, shake, quake with cold and fear and dread. My hour has come.* I feel something rising from deep within, becoming, taking form. I'm gagging, want to spit. Ahh – SPLAT!

'Fuckin' Hell!' He wipes the gelatinous, viscous substance from his head, stares at it dripping down his fingers. 'You gobbin' at me or sumfink?'

'What? Must be a leak somewhere.' Faces turned upwards, they search the ceiling as I laugh to myself. But I'm not finished. Oozing out of me comes more shimmering matter, a flow of white, luminous vomit, puking all over his face and body.

'What the fuck?' He jumps out of his seat, trying to wipe it off, whimpering like a maniac. His mate stands and edges away. 'Where's it coming from? It's disgusting!'

'Get it off me!' he screams, darting his head from side to side, looking in my direction and trembling. 'Leave me alone! What do you want with me?'

'Who you talkin' to mate? There's no one there.'

You murdered me. Twenty-five years ago in this carriage you stabbed me to death. Now you're going to pay. Confess or go mad!

'No. Keep away. Leave me alone!'

'What's got into you, man? You're bonkers.' We've entered a station. The doors open. The killer's companion exits by a far door. Blood is dripping from my knife wound; my eyes fix my murderer like a pin fixing a specimen to a tray. I raise my hand and point an accusing finger. *You'll never escape.*

'HELP!' He backs out of the door, the stuff I've deposited on him disintegrating as he clears the car. The doors close and he runs screaming down the platform. With an immense feeling of relief I look around. The remaining passengers stare out the windows open-mouthed at the retreating figure, then turn to each other, murmuring.

I'm light-hearted and triumphant. I've done it! Ectoplasmic manifestation. More than that, I've faced the full horror of my violent death, and come to terms with it. What an exertion! I'm exhausted. Another station's gone by; where are we? Coming up to Edgware Road. I'm no longer afraid. Darkness is descending upon me. Should I resist or surrender to it, give myself up to the universal consciousness? Is this the final release, the end of the line, or the beginning of another journey? Must I wake again at High Street Ken, or shall I at last be free?

151

BEYOND THE GRAVE?

Donald West

Young Helen had a problem. She considered herself an independent, modern-minded woman, in contrast to her old-fashioned parents. Born in Poland, they were devout, conservative Roman Catholics, regular church attenders, and proud of their respectability. Her boyfriend Arthur was an argumentative atheist, a strong supporter of a local humanist group, and fond of citing Richard Dawkins' *The God Delusion*. When she brought him home to introduce him to her parents, on hearing mention of the church, he launched into a tirade against religion, from the violence of the crusades and the horrors of the inquisition to the prohibition of contraception and the persecution of gays.

Arthur was well educated, but as a freelance artist his income was uncertain. Moreover, his father, a successful market stall holder, whose earnings had supported Arthur at art school, was, in Helen's parents' eyes, undeniably working-class. They considered him a very disappointing choice as a prospective husband for their precious only child. Helen's mother was about to have radical surgery for breast cancer, so it was a bad time for an additional emotional upset about her daughter's intentions.

Helen was in love and would not let the situation prevent her from accepting an invitation for a weekend visit to Arthur's family, so she could get to know his parents. She found their free and easy hospitality enjoyable. The absence of stiff, polite small talk and self-conscious references to cultural visits to exhibitions and concerts that characterised the conversation when her parents received visitors, was a welcome change. She was amused, but not surprised because Arthur had warned her in advance, when his parents, despite their jovial acceptance of her relationship with their son, allocated to her a separate bedroom, while Arthur was to share with his brother.

Once settled in bed, Helen reached for the novel she had brought with her. She was halfway through the story and wanted to follow the narrative further. Before long she felt tired and bent over to lay the book down on the bedside table. As she straightened up she was amazed to see a man standing at the foot of the bed, in front of the wardrobe.

She realised immediately that he could not have entered the room in the normal way without her seeing him coming through the door. It was as if he had somehow emerged from the wardrobe. She had not yet turned off the light and could see him, or at least the top half of him, perfectly clearly. He was elderly, with a bushy beard, and wore a fur hat that made her think of Russia. The left side of his face was dark and seemed bloodstained. He nodded his head and gave a slight smile, seeming to express satisfaction. As the lips moved she noticed the glint of a gold tooth. Then he disappeared, or rather melted away, retreating backwards through the closed wardrobe door.

Being a rational person, she knew she must have had some kind of hallucination. That disturbed her. She had never experienced anything like this before and feared she could be losing her mind. She determined to reject the thought and try to get to sleep. In the morning she remembered the vision and described it to Arthur. She expected him to dismiss it as of no importance, just overactive imagination.This she would have found reassuring, but instead, he exclaimed 'That's extraordinary!'He went on to explain that the description fitted his maternal great-uncle, now deceased, who had been a visitor to the house, staying in that bedroom during vacations from his work as a lumber-jack in Vancouver. The beard, the port-wine birth mark that disfigured his left face, the gold tooth and the fur hat, appropriate to cold Canadian winters, confirmed the identity. Arthur

153

remembered that someone else who had slept in that room had reported feeling something strange.

That Arthur took her story so seriously, despite his strictly rational approach and his aversion to religion and superstition, worried Helen. She could not rid her mind of her strange experience. It was an irritating puzzle. Resorting to the internet, she located the website of the Society for Psychical Research and wrote to their address, asking for advice. In due course, Dr Heathwaite, a lady member of the organisation, telephoned and invited Helen to visit her at her home to discuss the matter. On arrival at the house, the doctor seemed a matter-of-fact person, not what Helen had expected of someone involved with matters supernatural. She listened quietly to Helen's account and began by explaining that Helen's experience was not exceptional and not something to be worried about.

'In fact surveys show that 10 per cent of the population, when questioned privately, admit to having at some time or other seen a realistic apparition, most often of an unrecognised figure that means nothing to them. There are various theories about these appearances. I have my own ideas, but my Society doesn't offer any official conclusion. We support research into these experiences and I can suggest some reading material.'

Helen's curiosity was aroused and she pressed for more information, saying 'Well, in my case, I didn't recognise the apparition, if that is what you call it, but my boyfriend says he knows who it was.'

'It is true that occasionally people believe they see in these visions someone they know, quite often someone dying or already dead. The spiritualist view is that apparitions are physical manifestations of the surviving spirit of a dead person. Of course this belief is totally at odds with science, which seems to show that our consciousness, memory and personality depend on a functioning brain, which dies and rots with the rest of us when we die.'

'If these are not spirits, what are they?'

'These visions have a phantom-like quality, appearing and disappearing mysteriously. They don't displace anything or leave a door open. They are most often seen when a person is alone and at rest. Any witness who might be present is unlikely to see it. They seem to be subjective experiences, best thought of as waking dreams. In fact apparitions are particularly liable to be seen when people are half asleep.'

'I am sure I was awake. In any case, how could I have dreamt about my boyfriend's uncle; I did not even know of his existence?'

'As in dreams, the vision is a personal construction, a wish fulfilment, for example. The thought came to you that the face was expressing satisfaction. Perhaps you were wishing for a sign of approval for your relationship with Arthur'.

Feeling she was not being taken seriously, Helen responded tartly: 'But I did not connect it with Arthur until he told me it was his uncle. And how could it be that Arthur found the figure was exactly like his great-uncle?'

'A resemblance is not beyond the bounds of coincidence, considering the great number of apparitions, most of which are quickly forgotten because they do not happen to coincide with anything. Then again, apparitions are spontaneous and ephemeral. They cannot be captured and preserved for analysis and experiment. They exist only in someone's recollection. Psychologists have shown that anecdotal evidence based on witness reports is untrustworthy. Suggestive questioning of a witness after an unexpected and emotional incident, such as a traffic accident or a séance room event, can induce false memories, versions of events that are wrong, although carrying absolute personal conviction. Perhaps Arthur's comments about his relative's appearance influenced your memory of the closeness of the resemblance.'

155

'I find that hard to understand. I told Arthur about the tooth and the red face without him having to question me about it.'

'I am only putting to you hypothetical possibilities. There are spiritualists who firmly believe in communication with the dead and they would no doubt argue that your experience was an example of a dead uncle, still aware of earthly matters, wanting to help, from beyond the grave, a nephew he still cared about. Of course more orthodox religious authorities, despite their faith in eternal life, do not believe in or approve of communication with the dead. As I said before, our society does not propagate an official line. People have to use their own judgement. I can let you have some literature on the subject, with many examples and analyses of experiences such as yours. There is some evidence that people who have these experiences score higher than average on psychological questionnaires measuring fantasy proneness and suggestibility. You should ask yourself how you would judge the matter if it were a story told you by someone else.'

On her way home Helen's initial reaction was one of annoyance. She knew quite well what she had seen and thought any other version of the event was impossible. She felt she was being disbelieved and unfairly accused of being an unreliable witness. She was certainly not going to let what happened alter her trust in Arthur's good sense.

With the passage of time, doubts set in and the incident began to feel less important. When she thought about it at all, her state of mind became much like that of Omar Khayyám, who, after frequenting doctor and saint and hearing great argument, came out the same door as in he went.

156

THE INN

Miles Martlett

It had been a long trek, and though I had thoroughly enjoyed the day's walking, my venturing off the beaten track having led me through some stunning scenery, more than anything I fancied a meal and a bed. But for some distance now I had seen nothing but barren landscape, and I was resigned to having to spend a night in the open. The sleeping-bag I always carried on these expeditions would keep me warm, but I had no food left and just a last few drops of water left in the bottle. Then I thought I saw a light in the distance. I stared at it for a few minutes, suspecting that it was some trick of the light, or a will-o-the-wisp, though I had thought these were confined to marshy areas where the rotting vegetation gave off the methane gas which had originally given rise to the belief that they were living creatures.

But apart from flickering slightly it stayed constant, so I forced my weary legs towards it, and was both surprised and delighted to stumble across a small hostelry of some sort – at least that was what I supposed it was, for a sign hung outside, swaying gently in the light breeze that had sprung up a little while before. In the dim light I couldn't make out what it said or what the painting on it referred to, but I was too tired to care, so I went up to it and pushed the door,

It required more effort than I had expected, but then when I did get it open I saw it was constructed from a thick piece of wood. Inside was what looked more like a private sitting-room than a bar or a hotel reception-room, while to the left of it was a sort of dining-room, but with just the one table, already laid.

In one of the easy-chairs was sitting a man who got up as I entered the room and came forward to me. 'Good evening, sir,' he greeted me. 'May I fetch you a cool drink?'

'That would be great,' I agreed as I sank into the chair he indicated for me, and a minute or so later he reappeared with a long glass which he handed to me, when I immediately took a long and very refreshing swig: I didn't know what it was: it tasted vaguely fruity, but with a richness which suggested it had some alcoholic content. Whatever it was, it was just what I needed.

The man waited till I had finished, then asked 'Would you like a bath before your dinner?'

At the back of my mind I registered that he was taking a lot for granted, but the prospect was so inviting that I put my doubts away and answered 'I'd love one.'

'If you would like to follow me, sir,' he suggested, and I obediently got up out of the chair, with a slight effort, and followed him up some stairs. At the top he opened a door, and there was a bathroom, but more surprising was the fact that it held a bath full of water. I could see that it was hot, for steam was rising from it, so I went in and started to strip off my clothes.

A minute later I was gratefully relaxing in the bath. I hadn't realised just how tense I had been until I was lying in the steaming hot water, and I allowed myself the luxury of a good long soak. When I finally got out, I saw a towel laid on the chair: my clothes had been removed, but there was a dressing-gown which I put on, and a pair of slippers, which fitted well. I went downstairs, feeling a new man, and was directed to the table, where a bowl of soup was immediately placed before me.

It was cold and refreshing, just the thing for the sort of hot weather I had experienced, I thought. While I was eating it, a bottle of wine was opened and put on the table, and when I had finished the soup and the plate was being removed, I poured myself a glass and held it to my nose. I didn't recognise the aroma, and when I sipped it I found the taste slightly strange at first, though by the second mouthful

158

my palate had adjusted to it. Meanwhile the next course had been laid before me. I was so hungry I felt I could have eaten anything, but in fact I enjoyed what I was given very much, though I would have been hard put to it to say exactly what it was I was eating.

But it was good, and after I had also eaten a dessert made of some sort of mixed fruits, I relaxed in the chair with a coffee and brandy. For the first time I looked more closely at the waiter: he was quite short and slightly built, with irregular features, and he didn't look to me as if he were a native of the region. But I was too tired to speculate any further, and by the time I had drunk the last of the coffee, I felt ready for bed. The waiter, presumably sensing this, led me upstairs and into a fair-sized bedroom with a bed temptingly made up. I threw off the dressing-gown, clambered into it gratefully, and in next to no time was asleep.

In the morning I awoke feeling full of beans and ready for what the day should prove to have in store. My clothes, neatly pressed, were waiting for me, while breakfast was laid when I went downstairs, and as I was in no hurry to leave such a hospitable inn, I lingered over my second cup of coffee. Finally, though, it was time to move on. I paid the surprisingly modest sum asked, adding a substantial tip, and as I left glanced up at the sign. In the broad daylight I could easily read 'The Weary Traveller,' and I thought how appropriate.

The painting beneath it, too, looked not unlike how I must have appeared when I arrived at the inn, and I smiled at the resemblance. When I was back home I told my friend Berwick how pleased I had been to come across it when I had practically given up hope of finding anywhere suitable, and he smiled one of his enigmatic smiles. I suspect that these are as much as anything to impress other people with all the strange things he knows, but anyway he said he would like to see it.

At the time I had thought that just a casual phrase, but when I was planning my next trekking holiday he expressed a desire to join me, and suggested I took him over the places I had visited on my last trip. I had been intending to visit an entirely different area, but under Berwick's persuasion I agreed to retrace my former route, though I was none too pleased. But Berwick is somehow difficult to refuse.

He is quite a strange man, with many even stranger interests, but though he is inclined to pontificate, he usually does know what he's talking about, so I accord his words more respect than I would admit to his face. I also enjoy his company, though it regularly, as on this occasion, means I end up doing what he wants rather than anything I had planned myself.

As a rule I tend to follow my fancy on these treks: though I of course do carry maps of the region I have chosen, I find it more interesting not to stick to well-worn routes, but follow where the whim of the moment leads me, and though more than once I have got lost, I have never had too much of a problem getting to my destination, however roundabout the journey should prove to have been.

This time, of course, I had to try and find exactly the same route as I had taken previously, and I had to rely to a considerable extent on my visual memory, which is not always totally accurate. So I wasn't entirely surprised when I failed to find the spot where I had come across the inn, and as Berwick knows me quite well, I imagine he wasn't all that surprised either.

Probably trying too hard to find it had led me further astray, for I found myself I didn't know where, but certainly far enough from the comforts of civilisation, and with none of the landmarks I remembered from my former trip that might indicate the inn was somewhere around. So I was more than a little surprised that, when I had stopped, fed up and unsure what to do, I noticed what looked like a familiar light flickering in the distance.

Berwick hadn't seen it, so I grabbed his arm and pointed to it, and we set off towards it. I was not entirely surprised to find it was an inn, almost certainly the same inn: at least there was the same sign blowing gently in the breeze, and the building looked as I remembered it. I glanced over at Berwick, then pushed the door and went inside.

It was the same, but different: when the waiter got up and came towards us as we entered, I saw that there were two places laid at the table. I looked at Berwick again, but he didn't seem particularly surprised. I hadn't realised that such a small place would boast two bathrooms, but we were both led upstairs at the same time, and there were two bedrooms as well.

Berwick seemed to have something on the tip of his tongue, but he didn't say anything till the next morning, when we had paid the bill and were leaving.Then he said cryptically 'I would advise you not to use that inn again: you might find it difficult to get away from.'

I asked him what he was going on about, but he just shook his head. Berwick is quite often like that: he comes out with these gnomic pronouncements, and refuses to elaborate on them, so I try not to take them too seriously. As we walked away, I looked up at the sign, perfectly still since there wasn't even a light breeze. To my surprise, it read 'The Weary Travellers', and the painting beneath showed two figures which bore more than a passing resemblance to Berwick and me.

I reassured myself it had to be a coincidence, but I decided that next year I would go somewhere entirely different.

COLOUR HIM GAY

Gail Morris

Working as an agency carer had its ups and downs, each day different, not knowing what you might find so you couldn't keep to schedule, much as the agency might nag. Mrs Bain might have fallen and you'd have to get the ambulance. Mr Mallow, with dementia, might keep you arguing on the doorstep: 'Who the hell are you, coming here – you're not washing me, you black cow' even though he saw you every day. Mrs Abraham's family distraught as newly released from hospital she lay inert, apparently dying, and they not knowing what to do.

We got minimum wage, had to pay our own petrol, no special parking permit so had to pay our own fines. On the plus side we were out and about. It was interesting meeting new people, seeing inside their houses, how they lived. Not so good seeing how they died. Miss Springer told me she'd arrange her own death – 'Don't worry about me, love. I can't afford Switzerland but I'll sort something out. Don't ask, the less you know the better.'

Miss Morrison was 'one of us'. I suppose being a lesbian she should have been 'Ms' but it was Miss on her notes. I could only guess at how many of our clients might be LGBT. Perhaps Mr Colman. Miss Morrison claimed she could tell in a trice. At 85 nothing got past her, she said. Knew me at once. 'It's in the eyes and the smile.' During training we were told to 'respect all lifestyles', code for LGBT. I came out subtly when I thought a client might be of what my friend Lee calls 'the higher faith' by mentioning a book or film, and it was a pleasure to see them relax. Of course sometimes they looked baffled. When I was right, their books and stories came out.

Imagine having to hide your own books from visitors. I'd never had to do that.

Miss Morrison told me she had a week at a holiday home for disabled people and had a whale of a time as nearly all the male staff were gay and made a big fuss of her. The other guests were puzzled: 'We can't understand why you get on so well with these boys.'

She was my favourite too. We bent the rules. I wasn't supposed to clean or shop but I did bits of both for her, and hanging curtains and so on. I was supposed to help her wash and prepare meals, but as she gradually became more capable of doing some herself we used the time for other things: taking out rubbish, replenishing food and water for the garden birds, or just having a chat over tea and the cakes I'd brought.

I still did her feet, of course, she couldn't manage them. I thought it important I still went there every day so she had a regular visitor, though she wore an alarm fob for emergencies.

Her friend's little boy Alec was dumped on her most afternoons but he was no company. He roamed round the garden or played with his toy cars on the patio. He was a bad stutterer and something on the autistic scale, she said. He liked to be ignored. When I waved a hand at him he hunched his shoulders and moved away. He was slender, in white T-shirt and dark jeans, pale-faced with pennants of straight black hair. Sometimes I put a cake or sandwich on the patio table for him. He could lie for a full half-hour on his back on the little bit of lawn, staring at the sky.

The long narrow back garden was divided into 'rooms' by means of trellises supporting honeysuckle and runner beans, to make it look larger. A mirror on the far wall augmented the effect, quite an intriguing playground for a quiet sort of child. Miss Morrison said 'I've told him to leave the slugs and snails for the hedgehog. Not that I know if I have one.'

There was a water feature, a tumble of red rock about two feet high with a gentle cascade of water to make a pleasant sound though, she said, 'When I first had it that noise made me want to pee and I thought of switching it off but now I hardly notice it.' Her equally elderly cousin Percy who created it came to service it, and his daughter Mary came twice a month to keep the garden in order.

Miss Morrison had a little triangular walking frame but when I was there we sat indoors with the back door open looking over the quiet garden where Alec flitted about. I said he must be lonely and she said 'Who knows? Autistics live in their own world, don't they? School must be torture for him.'

She was a great reader, she must have had a good thousand and threatened to leave them to me. Where could I put them in my little flat? I'd need to have a massive garage sale, only I haven't a garage. There was every subject under the sun, not only lesbian and gay: social studies, history, biographies of people I'd never heard of, poetry, travel, and a whole shelf on the occult, spiritualism and the afterlife.

She was sure she'd meet up again with Margery, her partner for forty years – 'All that time can't go for nothing' – though the single attempt to contact her wasn't satisfactory. 'I'll have something to say to her when we do meet, she left her papers in such a state, and why she squirrelled away the house insurance in the last place you'd expect, I don't know. But I suppose all the hassle of that took my mind off the grief a bit.'

She'd gone to a spiritualist meeting in hopes of obtaining useful information from Margery 'But it was useless, she only told me what I already knew: to cut back the tree peony. I could see for myself that needed doing.'

I didn't imagine I could achieve forty years with someone. Four years seemed my limit. Miss Morrison patted my hand. 'You'll find the right one. Lovely girl like you, you've still got it all ahead of you.'

Miss Morrison was tall, a little stooped, had a thin long face, not handsome but pleasing, pale blue eyes and her almost white hair pinned up. Her skirts were mid-calf length and she often wore a wrap-around apron. Margery, from the photos, was short, round and with a jolly mischievous smile. Margery had done the cooking and Miss Morrison said it was a while before she got the hang of it herself.

'One-pot cooking is my style. Bung in all the veg and put on low heat, what could be simpler.'

She was trying to become a vegan – 'It's never too late' – but occasionally gave way to her craving for cheese. I said I couldn't do as she did – 'I need my meat.'

'But it's not *your* meat, is it? It's the flesh and blood of that animal. Still, I can't talk, taking the milk from the mouths of calves.'

I told her of my plan to work in/help to establish a residential complex of LGBT elders. She laughed. 'There might be ructions. But sign me up for it if I'm still around.'

To this end I took a job in a care home to gain experience, so I was calling on Miss Morrison weekly or fortnightly only, though I still did a few chores for her. She said my replacement was adequate but 'She works by the book and isn't on our wavelength. Poor woman tells me all about her inconsiderate husband. I wonder if I could suggest she changes sides.'

My new job was challenging but it often seemed to me I was observing how things should *not* be done rather than how they should. For example, using a form of baby talk to people old enough to be their great-grandmothers. I felt they ought all to meet Miss Morrison.

New people moved in next door to her. Scaffolding went up in front and she told me 'Alec hasn't been for a few days. He hates any disturbance.'

I was surprised she still had him around. How old was he now? He'd been twelve when I first met him, I thought, a very young twelve.

'Seventeen,' she said. 'I'm concerned about him, naturally. He needs to be with his own kind, not with an old woman. Especially as he's gay. Perhaps you didn't notice. I could see it at a glance once he was thirteen.'

I tried to think. He'd always seemed a child to me and I hadn't seen much of him the last couple of years.

Miss Morrison poured tea and said calmly 'Of course you know he's a ghost.'

'What?'

'Oh yes. I thought you'd realised as you left him alone. You never saw his reflection in the garden mirror, did you?'

It would never have occurred to me to look for it, and when I was out there he usually wandered off behind a trellis.

I said 'But I've put out food for him. You asked me to.'

'Oh, the fox or magpies would have got that. It was just a courtesy, to make him feel at home.'

I tried to think. He hadn't looked insubstantial. For something to say I asked why she had named him Alec.

'That's his name. Alec Lattery. His mother used to clean for me, privately, before you came. Then one week, no Mrs Lattery. Next week she called to tell me he'd been killed in a horrible road accident. Poor soul. She poured it all out to me in the garden. He'd been here a few times; he'd play with his toy cars in the garden while she vacuumed. Very withdrawn because of his stammer and what not. She stayed about three hours that day talking about him, not weeping, just going over practically every detail of his life. Almost reliving his life. How he'd seemed an ordinary baby, then the signs that he was different and her not being believed. That hurt her a lot, as if she was imagining it or making it up. She thought he might have had some treatment earlier, though I don't know if there is any. I felt worn out listening to her by the end and she looked exhausted. I can tell you I had a couple of sherries when she'd gone. She couldn't bear to think he'd be forgotten. She'd been told she'd "come through it" and she said "but that's just forgetting, I don't want that".

'I had the feeling she thought *I* would forget and that's why she told me so much, like depositing an archive with me. She gave me one of his little cars. I told her I would always remember him and of course I have. A few weeks after the funeral he appeared.'

'Did you tell her?'

'No. She'd gone away She had other children but I suppose he was her special one.'

'Weren't you afraid seeing him? Or nervous?'

'Good heavens, no. You might ask why he's *here* and not with her. This garden is peaceful, or *was*' – with a glance next door – 'and there's the water feature. Running water creates a conducive atmosphere. Read T. C. Lethbridge.

'My theory is this: Mrs Lattery's intense grief and her retelling of his life, together with the aura of the moving water, drew him here, or recreated him, gave him form and impressed him on this place. And my own thoughts must have been influential. Well, I *know* they were. Usually ghosts stay the same age, don't they. But every year I say to him, in June, "Birthday time again, Alec, get a move on," and he does. He picks up a lot from me.' She paused and added bluntly 'I can see you think I'm mad.'

'No I don't. I saw him too. It's just occurred to me I never heard a sound from him.'

'Sometimes he sort of croons. I believe stutterers have no difficulty in singing; maybe I influenced him there too. Margery could explain better than I do. She was the one really interested in psychic matters. She said ghosts are affected and even shaped by being observed, and the more often seen the stronger the effect. We reinforce them, in other words. Hence the tendency for ghosts to be in costume. Clothes can't be spiritual *We* must be creating them somehow. In a way I made Alec what I wanted. I coloured him gay, if you like. Now it's a worry. There he is on his own. I won't be here forever. He needs to move on.'

I thought well, if *you* did it surely you could have given him a brighter T-shirt, but said 'Can't you make him disappear?'

She looked shocked. 'That would be like killing him! I'm surprised you suggest it. He's gone temporarily because of the racket next door. He went when I had the new boiler put in but he comes back. Now, talking of next door, and to prove my sanity, I want you to take them this, my best butternut bake. House-warming present. I glimpsed the husband and he looks nice. Tell them if they run short of anything they can always pop round but warn them I'm slow in answering the door.'

I went round with the neighbourly offering and as I introduced myself and the butternut bake to the young man he was joined by another. They were Barry and Tony. So much for Miss Morrison's gaydar. I've know several couples of this pattern, one dark and saturnine, the other a merry blond peach.

They invited me through to the kitchen, a journey hazardous with boxes.

'We're not unpacked as you see. These carpets are full of moth, we're having to get the lot out and put down laminate.'

I asked if that would be noisy – I have to say, more on Alec's account than Miss Morrison's.

'No, not at all, and you can tell Miss Morrison the scaffolding comes down this week. It was just the guttering and a bit of repointing needed done.'

Barry put his arm round Tony's shoulder. 'This is our first house together.'

I said I'd never have guessed, and we laughed.

Tony wanted to decant the bake into one of their own dishes. I said 'No hurry to give her dish back, she's loads of crockery.'

'Just as well,' said Tony, 'we'd probably have to search every box to find one. The person who packed the kitchen stuff' – he eyed Barry – 'didn't label a single box. A failure of literacy.'

Barry grinned and said, 'From what I can see of it through the fence, your friend has a nice garden. Lot of work to do here. All brambles.'

So it was, all overgrown dusty wilderness in comparison with Miss Morrison's oasis of greenery.

'What to do?' said Tony, 'I've only had window boxes till now.'

I don't know if I did the right thing. Time will tell. I said 'A water feature might be a start.'

WHITEBEECH

Brian Burton

Darren had practically forgotten that his father's side of the family even existed when he received a letter from a firm of solicitors informing him that Mr Claude Bascomb had died suddenly, leaving no male heir, and that Whitebeech, his Shropshire residence, passed to him as the nearest surviving male relative, plus the residue of the estate, amounting to just over twenty thousand pounds.

Darren was perfectly comfortable in his London flat, and certainly had no desire at all to live in Shropshire, but he supposed he could always sell it. However, a further communication from the solicitors dealing with Mr Bascomb's estate revealed that this was precisely what he could not do, since the property was entailed. It began to sound as if the legacy was a liability rather than a welcome gift, and he decided he had better take a look at it.

When he went into the office of the solicitors to collect the keys, he was asked if he intended to spend the night in the house, and when he answered in the affirmative, an older man came forward, introduced himself as Mr Whittinghame, the senior partner, and advised him against it.

Darren assumed he was saying the house would be damp and not prepared for his arrival, but instead he was informed that the place had acquired a doubtful reputation, since Mr Josiah Bascomb, Claude's father, had died in his bed there. His widow quite naturally refused to continue living there, but then only a few months later her son Claude, who had been going there at weekends, was found dead in similar circumstances.

'How old was Josiah?' Darren asked politely but sceptically, and was told that he was seventy-four at the time of his death.

'Quite a good innings,' Darren commented politely, but Mr Whittinghame shook his head. 'He was in excellent health at the time of his demise,' he asserted. 'Even so, it was, I would agree, not too surprising at his time of life. But when Mr Claude died only a few months later, that did give cause for comment.'

'It was something of a coincidence,' Darren agreed, 'but no doubt there was a perfectly simple straightforward reason for the two deaths.'

Mr Whittinghame, however, shook his head again, even more solemnly.

'The doctor said it was heart failure in both cases,' he informed Darren portentously. 'But he told me in confidence that it looked more like some form of asphyxia.'

'Asphyxia?' Darren repeated, somewhat bewildered. 'Was there a gas leak or something of that sort?'

'Nothing at all,' Mr Whittinghame assured Darren. 'He explained that he had put heart failure on the first death certificate because he couldn't see how it could be anything else. But when Claude Bascomb died in the same way, it was too much for him to swallow, and he performed an autopsy. Then he found signs of oxygen starvation, though he could detect no physical cause. No one was in the house when either of the deaths occurred, and there were no signs of any kind of breaking and entering, nor had anything been taken or even disturbed, so far as the police could tell.'

He was looking very serious, though Darren was inclined to think that he was making too much of it. But then he went on 'Needless to say, all sorts of wild rumours have been running around. I have heard since that it had once had the reputation of being haunted, though I was not aware of anything of the sort when the elder Mr Bascomb succeeded to it, and indeed it is only after the two deaths in such a short space of time that it has been mentioned, leading one to suspect a certain amount of invention.'

'Do you recall who lived there before Mr Josiah Bascomb?' Darren asked curiously.

'A sister and brother lived there for many years,' he was told. 'She died well into her seventies, but her brother lived to be ninety-three, and there was no suspicion of anything untoward about his passing. This has led me to feel doubtful about the tales of haunting since, though I didn't deal with their affairs, this is not a particularly large town, and I think I would have heard if there had been any such happening, or report of such.'

Darren nodded. 'I'll bear what you say in mind,' he assured the solicitor. 'Perhaps, in view of what you have told me, it might be wise to put up in a hotel for the night. Can you recommend one to me?'

After he had been duly furnished with the necessary details, he set off for the house. It was larger than he had somehow expected, standing in its own grounds, and hidden from the road by a substantial rhododendron planting, with a drive either side. He parked outside the front door and searched for the right key, which proved to be the biggest one on the bunch, large and chunky.

The door swung open noiselessly, disclosing a sizeable hall with a fairly imposing central staircase, the first feature to catch the attention, though afterwards it could be seen that there were several doors at the hall sides. The house smelt slightly damp, but not uncomfortably so: nonetheless, Darren agreed it probably wouldn't be a good idea to spend the night there, since the bedding wouldn't have been aired even if there were no unwanted guests to worry about.

He decided to look round the place before making any decisions, and he started upstairs, with a slightly morbid desire to see the bedroom in which the two men had died. Almost certainly it was the first one he looked into, since it had a four-poster bed and was fully made up. There was certainly nothing to suggest that it had been the scene of two suspicious deaths, which Darren found slightly disappointing in a way. Then he looked in the other rooms, but found nothing to rouse any particular interest, and it was with a vague feeling of anti-climax that he descended the stairs. An exploration of the ground floor again revealed nothing of note, but he told himself he was being silly in expecting to find anything out of the ordinary.

Once he had returned home, he phoned up the solicitors and spoke to the senior Mr Whittinghame again, asking him what sort of stories had been circulating about hauntings. But it seemed that Mr Whittinghame considered it unwise, almost improper, for a solicitor to pay any attention to that sort of tale, and so he had no real information to offer, and when Darren asked if he could suggest anyone who might be able to be more informative, the solicitor clammed up and said he had no idea.

Darren had never manifested any psychic abilities or sensitivity, so though he had felt nothing threatening or unpleasant in the house's atmosphere, he thought it might be a good idea to ask a friend of his, Simon Delancey, who was more on that sort of wavelength, to look the place over.

A few weeks later Darren returned with Simon, who had cherished a mild fancy for Darren ever since he met him, three or four years earlier, and was delighted to be able to use his powers, which previously Darren had rather written off as of no interest, for Darren's benefit. There was always the hope that Darren might slip into his bed, though there he was deluding himself, for Darren's preferences did not extend to Simon's slightly fey type of personality.

Simon looked at the house with interest as Darren drove them up to the front, commenting 'Very imposing. You've fallen on your feet here, my love.'

He would probably not have used that particular term of endearment if he had realised how much it grated on Darren, but as it was he carried on in blithe ignorance 'It must be worth a packet!'

173

'It probably is,' Darren agreed, rather less cheerfully. 'But as it's entailed, that's not of much use to me.'

'Oh!' Simon said, momentarily derailed, but soon rallying to continue 'there must be something you can do with it, though.'

'Give parties?' Darren suggested with a degree of sarcasm.

'It would be brilliant for that,' Simon agreed, oblivious to his host's less than enthusiastic response, as they entered the house and he gazed around at the hall. He was silent for a few minutes, presumably absorbing the atmosphere, then he announced 'There is something here, I can sense it. I don't feel threatened, though, and certainly I can't detect anything that would have caused the deaths you've mentioned. I think we can sleep here without worrying. But I'll go round the whole place first to be sure.'

The two of them went over the premises, with Simon paying particular attention to the main bedroom, where the two Bascombs had died, but without sensing anything inimical. Finally he had given the house the all-clear, and so they prepared to spend the night in it, Darren in the main bedroom, and Simon in one of the guest rooms, both of them having had the fire lit and the bed-linen aired.

In spite of Simon's assurances, Darren didn't feel altogether comfortable in the bed where two previous owners of the house had perished, but he knew he had to prove, to himself as well as to all and sundry, that the deaths were just coincidence and there was no hoodoo on the place. None the less, it was well into the small hours before he finally dropped off, with the fire still glowing quite brightly, and a bedside lamp giving brighter illumination.

Once he managed to get to sleep, however, he slept right through the rest of the night, not waking till Simon knocked on his door and called out to him. He replied, after taking a few moments to come awake, then donned a

174

dressing-gown and went downstairs to organise some breakfast for them both.

He was sure he had dreamed, but he could remember nothing of whatever dreams he might have had. They didn't seem to have been bad ones, though, for there was no lingering sensation of fear or panic such as was often the aftermath of a nightmare. Simon, however, not only had dreams but was able to recall much of their substance. He refrained from going into any detail, however, since much of their content had been sexual, and he suspected that this had been prompted by sleeping in the same house as Darren, even if not in the same bed or even the same room.

Having got through the night with nothing untoward to report, Darren felt much more positive about the house, and for the first time began to think over its possibilities with something like excitement. He had made his money through property speculation, something he had fallen into more or less by accident, after the spectacular rise in house-prices had made a property he owned worth many times what he had paid for it, so he had plenty of free time and sufficient funds to indulge himself.

His first idea was to stage a house-party and see how it went. But then, with his usual eye for the commercial possibilities of anything he came across, he thought of running Whitebeech as a hotel, an idea quickly modified to bed-and-breakfast. In a fit of enthusiasm, he went through the house, checking on the supplies of linen, crockery, and so on, finding a fair amount, but unsurprisingly old-fashioned in style.

As he went around, the idea grew on him, and so some days later he took a builder there to see what needed to be done to bring the place into condition, and get some idea of how much it would cost. This proved to be rather less than he had been prepared for: no major problems were found, so that the main expense would be the installation of central heating.

Once he was seized by an idea, Darren didn't hang around, and a few months later saw him ready to open for business. He worked long and hard at putting together a sufficiently enticing advertisement, and when he was satisfied that he had got it right, or pretty much so, he placed a series in the national gay papers and magazines, since he had decided to explore whether he could do enough business catering to an exclusively gay clientele.

Mrs Williamson, who had acted as Claude's housekeeper, was happy to perform the same service for Darren, even when he explained about the bed-and-breakfast guests he was hoping for. Though she didn't realise it, she had a double function: besides her ordinary duties, she was there to give a touch of atmosphere. Darren told her he had no objection to her recounting what had happened to the previous owners, and this was sufficient encouragement for her to retail the happenings to all the guests who would listen, while they gradually grew more sinister with each telling. This way the guests had the frisson of supernatural happenings without the inconvenience of actually experiencing them for themselves.

Apart from the housekeeper, he started off with only one other full-time member of staff, a lad, Timmy, who acted as waiter at breakfast and odd-job man the rest of the time. Darren had picked him from a number of applicants because, apart from being able to carry out the duties required, he was reasonably cute and ready to flirt with the guests.

Darren had never been involved in the hotel trade, and so he was quite surprised at the amount of bed-hopping indulged in by his guests. Timmy, however, who had been in the business since his schooldays, was much more worldly-wise, explaining to him that a considerable proportion of all hotel business centred round either this or the hiring of professionals. He also pointed out to him which guests seemed likely to have brought a hired escort or a toy-boy with them, and once his eyes had been opened Darren was usually able to tell for himself.

Then, when he was sure Darren wouldn't take it amiss, Timmy also explained to him that from time to time guests would ask him if he knew anyone who might be available.

'In Wokingham?' Darren exclaimed dismissively, but Timmy, with the accumulated knowledge of his twenty-six years, said 'There's always somebody, usually quite a lot of somebodies. Would you like me to see what I can find?'

Darren wondered to himself how he was going to set about it, but he refrained from asking and told him to go ahead.

Sure enough, a couple of weeks later, Timmy had found three young locals who were willing to do some part-time work. When Darren interviewed them, he stuck closely to their official duties, leaving it to Timmy to deal with the rest. He didn't think any of them were gay, and Timmy confirmed this impression later, while assuring him that they had no objection to earning something over and above their wages by lending themselves to a bit of the other.

Timmy had suggested that it would be a good idea to offer an evening meal, which would give a reason for the lads to make their presence known, and it was the waiters more than anything who made this a popular innovation.

Darren had imagined the lads would be embarrassed by the attention they received, but they seemed to flourish on the admiration and more that they excited. Before long the original three were joined by others, as word got around, and this in turn kept Darren's bookings up, though few of these new clients came for the peace and seclusion he offered in his advert.

Darren didn't make the mistake of thinking no one in the village would know what was going on, and he took pains to make himself some friends there. As he didn't have a bar, the landlords of the local pubs did well out of him: they were too canny to object to the influx of strangers, certainly not when their takings were considerably increased, and he also made sure to buy plenty of goods and local produce from the village shops.

He didn't have a particularly strong sex-drive himself, and he was somewhat amazed at the amount of sexual activity that went on under his roof. He commented on it to Timmy, asking whether it was usual in his experience, and Timmy agreed that it was more than he was used to, though he had never worked in an all-gay establishment, which he suggested might well be busier.

But then a professional psychic consultant booked a weekend, and before he left he took Darren on one side and told him what a wonderfully sexual atmosphere the house had. 'I'm not sure who it is,' he went on. 'I was myself too occupied to have attention to spare to investigate at all thoroughly, but you seem to have beneficent spirits of just the right kind for a gay establishment.'

Darren wasn't sure how seriously to take him, especially since his flowery manner didn't inspire confidence: on the other hand, if he mentioned this idea to others, it could only improve business, he knew. But he wondered why Simon hadn't picked up on this so-called atmosphere when he came down in the early days, and on impulse he phoned him and invited him down.

He didn't tell Simon that he was there basically as second opinion, and so he was quite impressed when he made similar comments. It was so different from the warnings he had received from his cousin's solicitor, not to mention Mrs Williamson's asseverations that the house carried a curse, that he was rather bewildered.

He asked Simon if he had any idea as to what was creating the effect, and Simon was calmly certain that the house was haunted, for want of a better word, by spirits who had this effect.

Darren wasn't even certain that he believed in ghosts, and certainly he had never heard of any kind of spirit visitor of the sort. Simon, however, informed him that they were far from unknown, though usually they were said to be active themselves rather than merely encouraging activity in others.

'Why on earth should they want to do that?' Darren asked. Simon had no idea, but suggested that the likeliest way of finding out was to look into the history of the house and see if it had any associations or past goings-on that might have served as the starting-point. But Darren had drawn a blank when he tried before, and so he didn't bother to follow this up.

When Timmy suggested that, once he had explained – and demonstrated – to the *soi-disant* waiters what would be expected of them, Darren should try them out, he was unable to resist the suggestion, though he contrived that Thomas was the first. He found him a particularly pleasant bed-companion, and would have been content to repeat the experience, but thought that he'd better try them all in turn to avoid any jealousy.

In general, what they lacked in experience they made up for with enthusiasm, he decided. He had thought going with them might possibly have a deleterious effect on their future attitude towards him, but it didn't work out that way: they were perhaps friendlier than they might otherwise have been, but apart from that there was no attempt to presume on what had happened between them by taking liberties or being unduly familiar. Thomas, however, would sometimes knock on his door when his services were not otherwise required, and Darren was never able to resist what was offered.

By this time the house was ticking over reasonably well, but most of the time it was operating at somewhere around half its total capacity, and Darren began to think about widening his catchment areas and taking mixed couples as well. He was already taking gay females, and there had been no problem with the gay guys over that, so it was no big step, he thought.

But it proved to be an unfortunate decision. From then on things started to go wrong. There was a subtle change in

179

the atmosphere of the house: before it had always seemed welcoming, though he hadn't noticed it, just taken it for granted. Nor had he realised, either, how lucky he had been that everything had run so smoothly until it stopped doing so. Breakages became more frequent, while the business of running the place started to become a chore instead of an enjoyable task, and not just for him, he soon noticed, but for his staff as well.

Similarly, he had taken for granted the aura of happy sexuality that had hung over the house. So many people had had enjoyable stays there while indulging in licit or illicit sex that the house had acquired a reputation as a good place to take one's partner, whether of the moment or something more permanent. But now that changed, and there were a number of arguments and quarrels, no doubt exacerbated by unsatisfactory sex.

He had arranged matters so that the straight and gay couples were accommodated in different parts where possible, and when he noticed that it seemed to be the straight couples who were affected, he thought at first it might be due to the rooms they had been placed in. But swapping gays and straights around made no difference, and he began to wonder if perhaps the women were sensitive to something in the atmosphere that passed over the men.

He had taken sufficient advance bookings for it not to be much of a problem at first, but unfortunately matters didn't improve. Couples would come down to breakfast subdued or ill-tempered, sometimes both. But it wasn't till some weeks later that one of the men asked to have a word with him and, when Darren had taken him into his little office, unburdened himself, in a shamefaced way but with determination, to say that he and his lady-friend had been plagued by ghosts,

Darren looked at him in something like stupefaction. 'Ghosts?' he echoed.

The man, Lance something-or-other – Darren always had a problem remembering their surnames – looked embarrassed but held his ground. 'Ghosts,' he repeated. 'What is more, puritanical ghosts.'

'Puritanical ghosts?' Darren repeated, even more at a loss.

'They only bothered us when we were – er, making love,' Lance explained bravely, doing his best not to appear embarrassed.

Darren looked at him uncomprehendingly. 'They were trying to discourage you from, er, getting together?' he asked.

Lance nodded. 'And me in particular. Miriam – my partner – wasn't bothered by them, but she could tell they were there, and she'll back me up.'

'You're saying there was more than one?' Darren was grasping at straws.

Lance nodded again. 'I think you'll find we're not the first couple it's happened to,' he added. 'I had heard vague rumours before I came, but I guess the others were too embarrassed to say anything to you – or has anyone else complained?'

Darren shook his head slowly. 'I don't understand it,' he complained. 'I've been sleeping here for months, often with company, and I've never experienced anything of the sort you mention.'

Lance nodded without interest. 'That's as may be,' he agreed perfunctorily. 'But you'd better try and do something about it. If it happens again tonight, I shall not be amused, and you can be certain that I shan't keep it to myself when I get back to town.'

And with that threat he got up and stalked out, leaving Darren wondering what the hell he could do. All he could think of was offer to put him and his partner in another room, and this was done, but, it seemed, to no avail, for the next morning Lance reported grimly that the same thing had happened as on the previous night.

181

Darren apologised profusely, for what good it did, but he soon found out that the word had indeed been put around, for his bookings dropped off sharply, only slightly augmented by a few who relished the idea of ghostly visitors, and deliberately sought the experience.

He talked the situation over with Simon, who had not been bothered by unwanted guests any more than he had. He realised that there had only been a problem when he started taking mixed couples, so it might be that the ghosts were antagonistic to females, though against that was the fact that only the male partners had been molested. It didn't seem to make much sense. Darren supposed he would have to go back to just taking gays, but he still wanted very much to understand what was going on, and the two of them agreed that their best hope lay in delving into the history of the house.

Mrs Williamson, when she arrived a little later, was clearly gloomily pleased that her warnings had been proved to have some basis, but she had no information to offer which was any help in getting to the bottom of the disturbances.

If the ghosts, or whatever they were, objected to the presence of females, one would have expected that they would have been the focus for the attacks. It didn't make sense, and Darren was at a loss what to do or what line of action he could pursue. Mrs Williamson had no knowledge of the houses' history beyond the last two Bascombs, and she didn't know of anyone who was better placed.

Darren tried the local library, but the librarian, a young girl who didn't even live particularly near, couldn't offer any help, and he was stymied. But about ten days later he had a phone call from a man who worked in the main library, in the nearby town. It seemed the girl he had spoken to had passed his request for information around, and the librarian in change of the reference section of the main library had managed to dig up some information about the house's early days.

It had originally been the centre-piece of a cluster of buildings, really a small estate. But over the years, as the family's fortunes declined, some parts had been sold off, others fallen into disrepair and been demolished, so that Whitebeech itself was now all that remained. Then during the eighteenth century it had come into the possession of one Phineas Bascomb, and being more commercially-minded than most of the family, he had thought over how to turn it into a source of income. He had no interest in living there himself, London life holding too great an attraction for him, and the house was rather too far from the town to run as a hotel or boarding-house. But being himself gay, and frequenting the molly-houses, as they were known in the slang of the period, he had hit on the idea of running it as a gay brothel.

So far as was known, he had taken no part in the day-to-day business, which was in the hands of a Mr Cook. It must have filled a need, for it was so successful that the authorities, no doubt scandalised by the presence of such an institution in their town – more accurately on the edge of their town – decided to do something about it, and one night it was raided and those present at the time arrested.

A number were brought to trial: Mr Cook was sentenced to the pillory, while four of the lads who worked there as whores were condemned to be hanged and the rest sentenced to transportation. None of the clients, however, appeared in the dock, an omission which caused much comment in the town, and it was loudly bruited that at least some of them were men of sufficient standing to be able to have their involvement hushed up.

Cook barely survived the pillory, and for a long time after that the house was left empty, Phineas having fled to the Continent. Gradually rumours began to spread about its being haunted, especially when a would-be burglar was found dead in one of the rooms, after which tales were recounted of strange noises and ghostly lights, though none of the tale-tellers ever claimed to have witnessed these events themselves: it was always someone else they had heard it from.

When Phineas died abroad, the house passed to his nephew, Silas, but he showed no interest in it, perhaps not wishing to be associated, even slightly, with a house of ill-fame. It wasn't till a good many years later that the then owner, Percy Bascomb, took a look at it and not only decided to do something with it but had the money to effect extensive repairs and alterations, with the house today essentially as he had remodelled it.

He, however, had not lived long enough to move into it when he retired, as he had planned, for he was stricken with a palsy and spent his few remaining years in his town apartment. His son had tried without success to rent it, and effectively shut it up, getting local people to keep an eye on it and attend to any essential repairs, and eventually he allowed his widowed sister to live there when her husband died.

It was his grandson, Josiah, who had decided to take up residence in the house, having, it was said, a fancy for acting the country squire. But for some reason he had found the place unwelcoming, though his wife had settled in quite happily, and it was she who had persuaded him to stay on.

'It was while,' the librarian told him in a confidential whisper, 'he was enjoying connubial bliss that he had a heart attack and collapsed. His wife, unsurprisingly, was so upset that she took against the house she had formerly liked, and refused to live there any longer.

'She had taken her two children with her, but her son, Claude, it seemed, hadn't been put off by his father's death, starting to use the house as a weekend retreat after the break-up of his marriage. But then he too died suddenly and the house, which had been entailed on the male line, passed to the nearest surviving male relative.'

It was with a certain wry amusement that Darren received the information that his house had once been used as a gay brothel. Although reasonably broad-minded, he

184

certainly would never have envisaged running that sort of establishment, but perhaps there was something in the atmosphere of the house, he reflected, that made him regard what went on more tolerantly than he would have before he moved there.

It certainly had a broader appeal than a reputation for being haunted, he thought, though none of what he had been told explained the deaths, unless of course they were entirely due to natural causes. Nothing in the librarian's sources of information made any reference to ghosts or the house being haunted, and he suspected that what he had been told when he originally moved in was largely if not entirely local invention.

But it seemed there were ghosts, and the most likely candidates were the four lads who had been hanged. It was pretty unbelievable that not that many years ago these four men had been executed for something so harmless as prostitution, but he recalled that female prostitutes in those times were regularly sentenced to be publicly whipped. It was some sort of possibility that the spirits of the four would harbour resentment against the folk who had treated them so harshly: perhaps they had it in, to put it vulgarly, for heterosexual men, or more likely heterosexual activity.

He had never heard of anything even remotely similar elsewhere, but he had to admit that neither he himself nor any of the gay men who had stayed there had received an unwelcome visitation; it had been more like some sort of encouragement. None of the part-timers, either, had had any problems, and Darren surmised that they wouldn't be molested so long as they didn't get up to any heterosexual antics on the premises.

It was still pretty hard to swallow, but he had nothing else to go on, so he regretfully decided to stop taking mixed couples and see what happened. After six months had passed with no recurrence of unwelcome visitations, he still couldn't quite believe it was because the spirits didn't mind, but on the other hand it seemed to be working, so he left it at that. Before long the place had become known as giving an extra meaning to the term 'gay-friendly', regaining its reputation as a good place to take someone you were interested in, and gradually the bookings built up to a more than satisfactory level.

Occasionally Darren toyed with the idea of asking one or other of the part-time staff to stay a night with a girl-friend, and see what was the result. But while all was going along smoothly, he decided it was more sensible to leave well alone.

TWELFTH NIGHT

Alice Windsor

'A contribution to the festivities,' Sylvia said, handing Iris a brown paper bag.

Iris opened the bag and took out a globe, about four inches in diameter, covered with small squares of mirror glass.

'A mirror ball,' Sylvia explained. 'You hang it up. Now don't call me Scrooge any more.'

'It's lovely,' said Iris. 'Where did you get it?'

'My cousin Adrian's stall. Dunno where he got it.'

'Maybe came from a disco,' said Iris. 'Think I'll put this up here in the shop, if that's okay. We've got plenty decs in the flat, but the shop does look a bit dismal.'

The shop was indeed lacking in Christmas spirit, its only decoration being two thin strands of tinsel, one gold, one magenta, straggling across the window.

'It's yours, do what you want with it,' said Sylvia. 'I take no further interest. I am not a Christian.'

'*I'm* not a Christian,' said Iris. 'I'm a pagan. We celebrate the winter solstice and the return of the sun.'

'Don't give me that,' said Sylvia. 'I've heard you bellowing "Hark the Herald Angels" along with the telly.'

'Why should the Christians have all the best tunes?' Iris replied, dragging the step ladder into the middle of the shop. 'Right here,' she said cheerfully, 'it can hang from that beam. I'll just go and get a hook.'

Sylvia admitted that the mirror ball did look nice, glittering away near the ceiling. 'I hope it's fixed securely,' she said anxiously, 'don't want it braining a customer.'

Iris assured her it was not about to come crashing down on anyone's head, and proceeded to give a lecture on the role of Christmas decorations in the continued existence of life on earth.

'You see, the lights and the colours in the middle of winter imitate the sun and encourage it to move back north and the days to lengthen,' she explained. 'Sympathetic magic. You've read *The Golden Bough*?'

'Um,' said Sylvia. 'I think it would anyway, don't you?'

'Actually not,' said Iris. 'At least not necessarily. Volcanoes, in – er – Iceland, sending up particles of – er – ash and stuff, staying up in the air, blocking off the sunlight, making winter last a year. Or maybe three years,' she continued vaguely, on shakier ground discussing volcanoes than sympathetic magic.

'If that happened, I hardly think a string of fairy lights would help,' Sylvia replied, locking up the shop. They went upstairs to their flat, which was dripping with tinsel, lights, holly and mistletoe.

Sylvia dreamed she was in the shop. She could see the window, with its scrawny tinsel strings glinting faintly in the light from the street lamps. She saw the door, locked and bolted, with the sign in the glass pane reading 'Closed'. That, she realised, meant it was displaying its 'Open' face to the street. That wouldn't do, in the middle of the night. She tried to walk to the door, to correct it, but found herself unable to do so. She could move her arms and legs, but when she tried to walk forward she met an invisible barrier. She couldn't turn round. She was trapped in the middle of the shop. A voice, not her own, whispered 'Help me.'

'Who's that?' she whispered back.

'Donna,' said the voice. 'Help me.'

'How?' asked Sylvia.

'Get me out of here.'

'I can't get *myself* out of here,' said Sylvia.

'Yes you can. Try.'

Sylvia tried. She moved her arse violently and kicked her feet against the invisible barrier. She woke suddenly,

188

her feet tangled in bedclothes and her hands punching the air.

Iris, in the bed beside her, was making very strange noises. Not the normal snorts and snores of a sleeping person; this was the sound of someone choking, struggling to breathe and about to give up the struggle. Sylvia leaned over and shook Iris, who did not wake nor react in any way. She shook her again, and this time Iris responded by stopping breathing altogether.

Sylvia, in a panic, ran to the window and opened it, then came back to the bed, grabbed Iris by her feet and dragged her over to the window. It was lucky that Iris was thin and Sylvia was strong. Sylvia managed to pull Iris's head up and push it out of the window, slapping her heavily on the back several times, everything she had ever heard about resuscitation techniques forgotten.

Despite this treatment, Iris gasped and began breathing wheezily.

'What happened? What am I doing out the window? Terrible dream,' she stammered. 'Couldn't breathe – hot, burning heat – choking – trying to get away – people *stamping* on me …'

Iris's dream seemed to have been worse than Sylvia's.

Sylvia led her back to the bed. 'Come on, you've got to get some sleep. You've got work in the morning,' she said gently.

'Last day before Christmas holiday,' Iris muttered.

'And I've got the shop to open,' Sylvia said, tucking the bedclothes comfortably around Iris.

Iris went off to work at 8.15 the next morning, leaving Sylvia to her usual leisurely breakfast of Marmite toast and mug of coffee. At nine o'clock she opened the shop.

Customers straggled in – quite a lot of customers, Sylvia was pleased to see. Looking for last-minute Christmas presents. Huh. Sylvia wore her helpful shop-assistant smile, inwardly feeling the smug pity of one who

189

had, as usual, completed her Christmas shopping in October. There were, of course, many seeking the Alan Bennett book and those she patiently directed to Waterstone's in the High Street. But there were enough wanting to buy a Harry Potter or the latest Stephen King to make a gratifying rustle in her till.

She had been quite prepared to stay open late had the public demanded it, but at five-thirty there was only one middle-aged man looking for *Pride and Prejudice.* For what seemed like the hundredth time that day, Sylvia explained that Spooky Books was a specialist shop devoted to books about the supernatural, fantasy, horror and science fiction. 'Waterstone's are staying open till seven,' she told him, 'you'll make it easily. Unless you'd like *Hitchhiker's Guide to the Galaxy* instead? Or *Lord of the Rings* maybe?'

No, neither of those would do. It was Austen or nothing. Sylvia locked the door behind him, remembering to turn the 'Closed' sign to face the street. She switched off the shop lights and hurried upstairs.

By nine o'clock the party in the flat above the shop was getting into its stride. The flat's sitting room was small, barely accommodating Sylvia and Iris's dozen or so friends. There would have been more room in the shop itself, but Sylvia, envisaging drinks carelessly knocked over on bookshelves ruining the stock, had refused to hold the party there.

Sylvia and Iris poured drinks, handed round snacks, chatted and laughed, but Sylvia was not feeling sociable. She had not recovered from the shock she had had when, after locking up the shop, she had gone upstairs to freshen up for the party. In the bathroom mirror she had seen, instead of the ruddy complexion, black hair and brown eyes that usually looked back at her, a thin pale face with long blonde hair and watery blue eyes. Sylvia had wiped drops of condensation from the mirror's surface, but the person in the mirror had not raised her hand. Instead she had whispered 'Please help me.'

'What?' Sylvia had said stupidly.

'I don't want to be here. None of us do. Want to move on. Break out. Help us break out …' The voice had trailed off, and the reflection had faded. Sylvia's own round face had appeared where it ought to be.

There had not been time to tell Iris about it before the guests had started arriving, and now Sylvia wondered if she ever would. Perhaps she had imagined it? It did seem it might have been the same person from her dream the previous night.

'"I'll get that,' Sylvia called, when the doorbell rang. That would be Silas, she thought.

'Hallo Silas,' she began, then stopped as the tall black man staggered back from the door.

'What the *hell* have you got here?' he asked. 'It's an *infestation.*'

He came back into the hall, more cautiously this time, and started up the stairs, followed by Sylvia.

In the flat, Silas looked around.

'It's not so strong up here,' he said. 'I think it's in the shop. Have you taken in any new stock? Second-hand stuff? Can I go and have a look?'

In the shop he stood still, looking and listening.

'Yes,' he said, 'in here. Many of them. Perhaps thirty or more.'

'Many *what*?' Sylvia asked. 'Ghosts?'

'Yes. Not malevolent. Young. Helpless. Hurt, trapped. We have to do something for them, Sylvia.'

'That's what she said. She kept asking for help. But I don't know how.'

'She?'

'She said her name was Donna. She's just a kid, about sixteen. I saw her in the mirror upstairs.'

Silas was walking around the shop, looking at the books, touching them, shaking his head.

191

'We haven't had any second-hand books in since October,' Sylvia said, 'and this only started last night.'

'We need to arrange something, to try to talk to them,' Silas said. 'Not tomorrow, it's the solstice, too dangerous; who knows what might come through if we open a channel then. And after that I have to go away, I promised to go up to Leeds to deal with a poltergeist. Look, I really don't think you're in any immediate danger here. If I did, I'd put off the poltergeist people and stay here till after Christmas.'

'No, that's okay, you go, we'll be all right.'

Sylvia regretted that more than once during the following week. On Boxing Day night she awoke to find Iris sitting up in bed, coughing and choking. Sylvia insisted asthmatic Iris should go and stay with her mother until Silas came back. Sylvia's dreams continued, and she began to see things in the daytime too: people, transparent wraiths milling about in all directions like water coming to the boil.

She opened the shop for the benefit of customers wanting to spend their Christmas book tokens, but business was slow. Hardly anybody seemed to want to stay in the shop long enough to find a book they might like to buy. One woman, rummaging hopefully in the children's section, was distracted by her four-year-old son tugging at her coat. 'Don't like it here, Mummy, all the big boys and girls, bumping into me, don't like it.' Mummy left without making a purchase, smiling apologetically at Sylvia and murmuring 'Be back when I've found someone to park him on.'

Sylvia locked up early on New Year's Eve and headed off for Iris's mother's house, where she saw in the New Year with the help of several glasses of Bailey's. She was easily persuaded to stay the night, and the next day returned to the shop, remaining only long enough to write a notice saying 'Closed Due To Illness' and sellotape it to the front door, before going back to Iris's mother's to spend the next few days in idleness and relative luxury.

'We've got to go back to the shop today,' Iris announced on the morning of 6th January. 'We need to get the decs down.'

'Oh for heaven's sake,' Sylvia protested, 'the effing place is *haunted*, and you're bothered about a few decs?'

'That's the point, no need to make it worse than it already is,' replied Iris.

The argument was interrupted by a telephone call from Silas, apologising for not having been in touch sooner – he had received several more offers of work in the Leeds area – and arranging to come to the shop that afternoon to see what he could do.

Iris's mother insisted on providing lunch before Iris and Sylvia set off for the shop, and by the time Iris had finished stripping the flat of its festive ornamentation, Silas had arrived in the shop downstairs.

He decided to start proceedings by attempting to communicate with the entities through a ouija board, and requested Sylvia's and Iris's help.

'Just a minute,' Iris called, detaching the skinny tinsel strings from the shop window. 'Only one more dec to take down, then I'm all yours.'

She hauled the ladder into the middle of the shop, and climbed up toward the mirror ball. Her right hand reached up and removed the loop of string from the hook in the beam, while she steadied the glass ball with her left. Suddenly she screamed, the ball fell to the floor and shattered, and Iris climbed down, whimpering with pain and holding her blistered left hand.

'It was red-hot,' she said to Sylvia, who grabbed her by the arm and hurried her to the cubby-hole kitchen area behind the shop, where she plunged Iris's hand into cold water.

Silas, alone in the shop, found himself surrounded by people, none of them seeming much over twenty years old, and dressed for a night out. They were screaming, and running in all directions, treading on fallen bodies.

Suddenly they were still, and silent, and one by one they disappeared. A movement at the edge of his field of vision caught Silas's attention. He went over to the ouija board in time to see the words spelled out: 'Thank you.'

Iris's hand healed without a scar, but nevertheless Sylvia had words with Adrian regarding the palming off of fire salvage stock under the guise of Christmas presents, making it clear it was not to happen again.

About the authors

Kathryn Bell was born in Glasgow and now lives in East London. She has been writing short stories for about twenty-five years, and has been published in *Sappho*, *Capital Gay*, *Gazebo*, and *The Green Queen*. She would like to write a novel but lacks the stamina. She enjoys folk music, chocolate, and arguing.

Brian Burton at one time supplemented an otherwise dubious income by casting horoscopes for those desirous of peering behind the veil. Nowadays, however, he panders to different palates with works of lowbrow fiction.

Jeffrey Doorn's previous work has appeared in *Gawp and Gaze*, *Queer Words*, *Gazebo*, and *Mandate*. Jeff was born and educated in New Jersey, USA. For the past 25 years he has lived in South London with his partner Stephen. Jeff's other activities include acting and directing plays, besides organising art shows and cultural events.

Michael Ewers has been writing for pleasure for over ten years; firstly science-fiction fantasy novels, then a series of novellas, followed by short stories. More recently, he contributes a regular column, articles and reviews for *Out & Proud*, a quarterly publication produced by Flag Powys. While he has had a novel-size sci-fi adventure available electronically online for over a year, this is his first book publication.

Martin Foreman is the author of several works of fiction, nonfiction and drama, including *First and Fiftieth* from Paradise Press. He runs Arbery Books, an online business specialising in rare books and ephemerar of gay, lesbian and transgender interest. Born in Scotland, Martin has lived in several countries and is currently based in London. More details on his website: www.martinforeman.com.

Michael Harth has been an avid reader of science fiction all his life, but mainly prefers to write fantasy. He has recently edited two Paradise Press anthologies, *Best of Gazebo* and *Eros at Large* and is currently engaged on a novel with supernatural elements and a young gay vicar as protagonist.

Miles Martlett spent most of his life trying to find a job that he could at least partly enjoy while earning a modest stipend. His eventual solution would not have received parental approval, but it taught him a lot about human nature. This led to a brief period as a guru, but when his disciples proved, for some incomprehensible reason, unwilling to take his every utterance as gospel, he decided to make his wisdom available to all in the form of a novel, which he hopes to finish this year. No doubt, in the approved manner, a workbook will follow.

Gail Morris, when not writing short stories, is given up to domesticity: gardening, cooking, and sewing but NOT cleaning! She is interested in the paranormal, UFOs, birds and Elvis Presley, not necessarily in that order. She lives in London and hopes never to leave it.

Anne Stanesby lives in South London. She is a retired solicitor who has written various published handbooks in the field of legal advice, while in 1989 her short story 'Non-custodial Sentence 7' was included in an anthology of original crime stories: *Reader I Murdered him*, published by the Women's Press. In recent years she has spent a lot of time pursuing her interest in horticulture, and the ideas for the two stories in this collection reflect that aspect of her life experiences.

Frank Storm was born in 1940 in Batavia, the then capital of the Dutch East Indies, now called Jakarta. Moved to Spain where he found more time to write.

Elsa Wallace lived in Africa for the first 30 years of her life, and has been writing for 40 years, mostly short stories. Her favourite authors are Ivy Compton Burnett and Dickens. Interests are human and animal welfare, veganism, ghosts, and tapestry. She works with a number of lesbian and gay groups.

Donald West – Criminologist, psychiatrist and one-time president of the Society for Psychical Research, since joining Gay Authors' Workshop has taken to writing short stories influenced by personal experiences.

Alice Windsor was born in 1969, travelling and working in the Middle East and Africa before settling down to a desk job in London, where she lives with her girlfriend and cat in a small house not unlike the one in the story, but without the ghost. She has been writing off and on as long as she can remember, but this is her first published story.

Lightning Source UK Ltd.
Milton Keynes UK
UKOW03f0840250713

214371UK00001B/3/P